"Are they mine?"

Valentina didn't answer.

"Valentina? Are they mine?" Cash asked again.

"Yes."

Realizing she hadn't expressed her gratitude yet for him saving her and their daughters, she murmured, "Thank you."

"Are you thanking me for them?"

"I'm thanking you for saving them. And me. That was... That could have..."

"It's probably my fault that you're in danger," he said. "That text..."

"Did it specifically threaten me? Us?"

He shook his head. "It didn't mention *them* at all. Just my ex-wife..."

"Tell me what it said."

He hesitated.

"I have a right to know, since it mentions me."

"I had a right to know about them," he replied, his voice gruff with anger.

"Yes, you did," she conceded.

"Why didn't you tell me?"

"Because you didn't want them."

"I didn't know—"

"You didn't want to be a father. You made that very clear to me. And when you had your lawyer serve me with divorce papers, you made it very clear that you didn't want to be a husband, either. All you wanted was your job."

"That's not true. I did want you, all the time..."

Dear Reader,

I am honored to be part of this Colton continuity series with so many fabulous authors! The Coltons of New York has it all: an exciting city, the danger of serial killers and, my favorite element, family. I have a big family myself, so I understand the Colton dynamics so well.

The hero in my book, Cash Colton, is about to learn that he has more family than he realized. His total focus since his divorce has been on his job, on catching serial killers. Even during his marriage, he spent too much time at work; that was why he wound up divorced. He couldn't give his wife what she wanted. When the Landmark Serial Killer sends him a text about his ex-wife, he's compelled to check on her and make sure she's all right. What he finds turns his whole world upside down...like he's on one of the rides at Luna Park on Coney Island, where Valentina Acosta Colton lives with two little girls: twins. His twin daughters. And they're all in much more danger than he even suspected. Valentina and Cash have to put aside their old differences to work together to keep their daughters safe. I hope you enjoy reading about them as much as I enjoyed writing about them.

Happy reading!

Lisa Childs

PROTECTING COLTON'S SECRET DAUGHTERS

Lisa Childs

HARLEQUIN

ROMANTIC
SUSPENSE

Special thanks and acknowledgment are given to Lisa Childs
for her contribution to The Coltons of New York miniseries.

Recycling programs
for this product may
not exist in your area.

ISBN-13: 978-1-335-59374-0

Protecting Colton's Secret Daughters

Copyright © 2023 by Harlequin Enterprises ULC

For questions and comments about the quality of this book,
please contact us at CustomerService@Harlequin.com.

Harlequin Enterprises ULC
22 Adelaide St. West, 41st Floor
Toronto, Ontario M5H 4E3, Canada
www.Harlequin.com

Printed in U.S.A.

New York Times and *USA TODAY* bestselling, award-winning author **Lisa Childs** has written more than eighty-five novels. Published in twenty countries, she's also appeared on the *Publishers Weekly*, Barnes & Noble and Nielsen Top 100 bestseller lists. Lisa writes contemporary romance, romantic suspense, paranormal and women's fiction. She's a wife, mom, bonus mom, avid reader and less avid runner. Readers can reach her through Facebook or her website, www.lisachilds.com.

With great appreciation for Patience Bloom, for including me in this continuity and for letting me continue my Bachelor Bodyguards and Hotshot Heroes series. Thank you so much for supporting the series and the characters I love to write!

Chapter 1

Since the killings had begun, FBI special agent Cash Colton had spent more time at the Manhattan field office than he had anywhere else, so it felt strange to be outside now. Well, inside an SUV driving toward Coney Island, but it wasn't the office or a crime scene, which was the only other place he'd been besides his office.

At least Coney Island wasn't a crime scene yet. But after the text he'd received, the text that haunted him, Cash couldn't help fearing that he might be heading to the site of another murder soon and not just because of the way the killer kept killing. That fear, because of that damned text, compelled him to make the trip to Coney Island to make sure *she* was okay.

Even before receiving that text, he'd been as

determined as the rest of his special unit to catch the Landmark serial killer. The first victim, Mark Wheden, had been shot in Central Park, and found with a typed note stuffed in his pocket: *Until the brilliant and beautiful Maeve O'Leary is freed, I will kill in her honor and name. M down, A up next.*

Like this lunatic actually expected them to free a serial killer because of his threats? Then there would be two serial killers terrorizing New York—although Maeve hadn't limited her killing to just the Empire State. She'd killed wherever and whomever she'd married. She'd also tried to kill a lover's wife in order to inherit that woman's fortune. Anything for money...

Insatiable greed was Maeve's motive for murder.

Why was the Landmark Killer killing? What was his motive? Had Maeve somehow brainwashed him the way she had that poor psychiatrist? Like she had all her husbands?

But even she had to see that there was no way she was getting released; she was being held in custody without bail because of all the murders she'd committed and the likelihood she would flee.

That hadn't stopped her admirer, though. The Landmark Killer's second victim, Andrew Capowski, had been found on the Empire State Building observation deck with a typed note in his pocket that had read nearly the same as the first but the second line said: *MA down, E up.*

Not long after that, a man named Edward Pendleton was murdered after leaving the Metropolitan Museum of Art. The next attempt had been on Broadway, but that victim had fortunately survived. Unfortunately, since his assailant had worn a mask and a hoodie, he hadn't been able to provide much more than a vague description. Male, maybe on the younger side...

The fact that the killer had been sending the Coltons personal texts told Cash and his team one thing: the killer was probably closer than they'd realized. Closer to them than they were to finding him.

He had to be stopped before anyone else died, and before anyone else was threatened. The way Valentina had been threatened...

Maybe she hadn't been named specifically, but the threat had been implied in the text Cash had received; he was the latest one singled out on the FBI serial killer team. His twin had been the first to be taunted.

Who the hell was it? Was it someone close to them as they had come to suspect? Someone within the FBI or within the Ninety-Eighth Precinct that had worked to hunt down the Black Widow serial killer, Maeve O'Leary? Someone who'd come to admire her for some sick reason?

The note about Valentina had been a text sent to Cash's phone after the first victim was shot on Broadway. No worries. Lots where that dippy actor came from. Tsk-tsk, Cash—murdered daddy and a sad ex-wife.

Instead of trying for another actor, the killer had

claimed the life of an assistant theater director after that text. And what about Valentina?

Was she in danger? Had that text been meant as an actual threat or was it just a ploy to distract Cash from the case? While it likely was a ploy, Cash wasn't immune to the text. It had worked. He *was* distracted. He couldn't stop worrying about Valentina even though he'd told a friend at the local police precinct about the note and had asked Sergeant Dave Percell to watch out for her, to make sure that nobody was lurking around her, trying to hurt her.

Was she really sad?

Why?

She couldn't still be unhappy about their divorce. More than three years had passed since Cash had set her free to have what she'd really wanted: a husband who wasn't consumed with his work and most especially one who wanted children. More than anything else, more than him, Valentina had wanted a family.

Because Cash hadn't been able to see how he could handle his career, marriage and fatherhood, he'd done what he'd thought would make Valentina the happiest. After she'd moved out to get some space from him, he'd filed for divorce. He'd wanted her to have the happiness she deserved. So why wasn't she happy? Or was the texter lying about that?

He hadn't lied about Cash's murdered daddy. That had happened; a serial killer was responsible for Cash's cop father losing his life.

And inadvertently responsible for Cash and all his siblings going into law enforcement.

So since he'd told the truth about that, he might have been right about Valentina as well. But how would the Landmark Killer know if Cash's ex-wife was happy or sad unless he'd gotten close to her? Did he know her? Or had he been stalking her like he had the victims whose lives he'd taken?

Those worries kept Cash awake at night, kept him on edge. Even though his buddy Dave at the local precinct had promised to keep an eye on her, Cash had also called Valentina to let her know about that text. To make sure she was aware of the potential threat. She'd been short with him, as if he'd caught her at a bad time. And maybe he had…

And ever since he'd heard her voice, he hadn't been able to get it out of his mind. Just as he'd never gotten Valentina Acosta completely out of his heart. Cash suspected that the Landmark Killer had known that when he'd sent Cash that text. He'd known how badly it would bother him, so somehow he knew Cash.

Maybe better than Cash knew himself, because in the past three years he hadn't let himself admit how he felt about Valentina. He rarely let himself think about her at all. If not for that damn text…

And then that call he'd made to her, to the same cell number she'd always had. Brennan had offered to make the call for him, as if it was somehow his fault that Cash had received the text even though their entire unit was hunting this sick serial killer. But he'd sent Brennan the first text: *Shouldn't you be out looking for me skulking around Broadway* theaters instead of shacking up with a murder suspect? I thought you Coltons didn't like killers because of what happened to poor Daddy.

Brennan had been reluctant to share the text with them. Probably because of the shacking up part. Cash smiled and caught a glimpse of his own reflection in the rearview mirror. Despite being twins, he and Brennan looked nothing alike because they were fraternal, not identical. Brennan had pale blond hair and pale blue eyes and a baby face while Cash had brown hair and green eyes and always looked like he needed a shave even if he'd just shaved. But given how busy he was, he'd given up and wore a beard now.

Valentina had always told him that she thought his scruff was sexy. But that was when he'd kept his beard neatly trimmed. He didn't look neat now. He probably should have stopped home and showered after leaving the office, but for some reason he'd had this compulsion to drive to Brooklyn and Coney Island. To see for himself that Valentina was really all right, that she was safe and not sad.

"Valentina? Are you all right?"

The voice startled her, drawing her attention back to the present, and not the past where it had been constantly slipping since that call a week ago. From Cash…

She had not heard the sound of his deep voice in three years, but she'd immediately recognized the rumble of it in her ear, raising goose bumps on her skin like they were rising now despite the warmth of the library.

"Valentina…" he'd murmured.

"Valentina!" the older woman repeated. "Are you all right?"

She shook her head and blinked and squinted against the late-afternoon sun pouring through the tall windows. Then she tried to focus on the woman standing in front of her, blocking her path as Valentina tried to push the double-wide stroller between the rows of children's books.

"You're not all right," Mrs. Miller remarked, and she reached over the top of the stroller to pat Valentina's hand. "What's troubling you, honey?" The back of the woman's hand had thick veins crisscrossing it, and on every finger, below the swollen knuckle, she wore a ring with big stones that sparkled and reflected the sunlight. The sun also glinted off the jewels hanging from the chains around her neck.

Four pudgy little hands stretched out from the stroller, reaching toward those shiny pendants. The girls loved shiny things.

She smiled. "Nothing, Mrs. Miller, I'm fine. Really."

The woman stepped back then and leaned down to smile at the toddlers in the stroller. "How could you not be happy all the time with these two gorgeous girls?"

Mother's pride suffused Valentina. "I just picked them up from day care." If they didn't love going to school, as they called it, she might have regretted having to work full-time. But as a single mother, she didn't have a choice. At least she had a job that she enjoyed.

"And you came right back to work?" Mrs. Miller asked with surprise.

"We're picking out a book for bedtime. Well, two books. They each get to choose one."

"You're passing your librarian's love for books on to your little girls, that's wonderful," Mrs. Miller enthused. "And speaking of books…"

"I tracked down that memoir you've been looking for," Valentina assured her.

"That's wonderful!" the woman exclaimed, her pale blue eyes sparkling like her rings with excitement.

"I ordered it to be sent here from the branch where I found it. If it arrives while I'm off this weekend, I asked Randall to call you and let you know," Valentina said.

"I can wait until you're back on Monday, honey," the woman said. "Then you and I can discuss it."

That was one of the parts of Valentina's job that she enjoyed most. Discussing books with other avid readers.

The older woman loved reading the memoirs of famous theater actors and actresses and socialites and artists from years past, probably looking for a mention of herself. She'd once been an actress before marrying well and becoming a socialite; there was even a rumor that she had also been a famous artist's model and muse.

"When are you going to write your memoir?"

Valentina asked. "Yours is the book I would love to read."

The older woman blushed and giggled and waved a hand in front of her face, and the sunlight glinted off the bright stones on her rings. She had the air about her, with the furs she wore and her perfect makeup and clothes and jewelry, of old Hollywood glamour. "I might be scribbling down a few notes here and there," she admitted with a sly smile. "But I find myself focusing on other far more interesting people and events than myself. I'm definitely not the type to kiss and tell. But I certainly enjoy reading the stories from the people who do."

Valentina laughed now, and the girls echoed it, despite having no idea what she was laughing about.

Mrs. Miller giggled again, and she looked much younger than her probably eighty or ninety years. "You enjoy your bedtime stories," she told them, and she patted Valentina's hand again as she walked past them.

The little girls leaned out either side of the stroller and stared after the older woman.

"Sparky..." Luciana murmured.

"Sparky," Ana repeated.

They must have been talking about the older woman's jewelry. Valentina smiled as her heart filled with love. They were so adorable with brown curls framing their little faces. Ana had dark eyes, like Valentina, while Luci's were green, like...

No. She wasn't going to think about him anymore. And for the next while, she managed that while helping the girls pick out books. But they knew the routine, so they chose quickly once they ruled out the ones they'd already read. Then they checked out and were back in the stroller, heading toward home, shortly after Mrs. Miller left.

The distance between the library and the high-rise condo complex where they lived was far enough that it was easier and safer to push the girls in their double stroller than for them to walk. The only problem was that with the street noise from traffic echoing off the commercial buildings, Valentina couldn't hear all of their chatter. Not that she understood much of it; they had their own little twin language. While they always understood each other, it wasn't as easy for Valentina all the time.

She still wasn't certain she understood Cash's call, either. He'd received a text about her from a serial killer? Or so he and the rest of his unit suspected, but nobody at the FBI had been able to trace it. With all their technology, how was that possible?

And why send Cash a text about her?

She had not had any contact with her ex-husband since that day she'd moved out to take some time to think, to figure out if she could accept what he was willing to give her. Whatever time that was left over from the job that consumed him. But she'd wanted more than that; she'd wanted a family. And that was the one thing he'd told her he would not give her. But he actually had…

Neither of them had known it when she'd moved out, though. She hadn't even known it yet when the divorce papers had come. Thinking he didn't care enough to figure out a compromise with her, Valentina had just signed them and ended it without an argument, without a fight. And she'd thought it was done, that she would never see or hear from him again. And she hadn't for three years…

Until that night a week ago.

"Valentina…"

And just the sound of his deep, rumbly voice had all the feelings rushing back, overwhelmingly intense. The pain, the loss, the guilt…

She should have told him all those years ago when she'd first found out herself that she was pregnant. But she'd figured that it was too late then, because she had already signed the divorce papers. And in sending them, Cash had clearly also been sending her the message that there was no hope for them as a couple. They were over. Done. He hadn't wanted the same things she had. He certainly hadn't wanted—

A loud pop rang out, startling her and making her jump. It wasn't so much the noise, which must have been a backfiring car that had passed or started up along the curb or in one of the alleys they'd passed. It was that she'd been so distracted again that she hadn't even realized where she was. That she had almost walked past the street she needed to turn on and cross to head home. She had to put that phone call out of her mind.

Cash hadn't called again. And he probably wouldn't. She knew he was busy chasing another killer, like he always was. The Landmark Killer.

She'd watched the news and had read the article the *New York Wire* had recently run about the investigation.

That article had been more about the investigators than anything else. It had been about the Coltons, who worked in the elite serial killer unit of the FBI. And it had revealed the reason why they were all on that unit and so dedicated to hunting down killers: because a serial killer had murdered their police officer father, to some of the investigators like Cash and uncle to a couple others, so many years ago.

But were they hunting the Landmark Killer or was he hunting them with the notes he left in his victims' pockets and with the text he'd sent Cash?

She didn't know exactly what the text had said, just that it had mentioned her. Since she and Cash had had no contact since their divorce, how had this serial killer known about her at all?

So was she in danger? And the girls?

Or were Cash and his siblings really the ones who were in danger, and the serial killer was just texting to taunt them as he had with those notes he left on his victims?

He had killed again.

Like he had so many times before. That didn't even bother him anymore.

Taking a life.

It wasn't a big deal. It was just what he did like other guys played video games. But this wasn't a game to him. It was a vocation.

One he had to protect at all costs.

This time he couldn't be certain that he wouldn't get caught. He couldn't be certain unless he *made* certain. He had to eliminate any possibility of being identified as the killer.

So he settled into the driver's seat and pulled the mask over his face and drew up his hood, pulling it tight around that mask so that nothing of his face reflected back at him from the rearview mirror. Nothing but his eyes: his cold, dark eyes.

Chapter 2

Cash knew Valentina's address. She'd given it to him to forward her mail after she'd moved out of the apartment they'd shared in Manhattan. She'd moved to Coney Island, into the condo where her grandparents used to live. Her grandparents, knowing how much their only granddaughter had loved visiting them there, left the condo to her in their will when they'd passed away shortly before Cash and Valentina's divorce. Valentina had wanted to move out there then while Cash had wanted to stay close to the Manhattan office.

Maybe losing so much of her family had made Valentina even more desperate to start one of her own. That was when she'd really started pressuring Cash into having kids, and she'd wanted to raise her children in a place she remembered so fondly from her own childhood. Cash didn't have that many fond memories of his childhood; his father's brutal murder had overshadowed all the happy ones.

It overshadowed his adulthood, leading him to a life in law enforcement. With his job consuming so much of his time and attention, he shouldn't have become a husband, let alone a father.

Valentina had often told him, during the three years that they'd been married, that she'd felt like a mistress, and his career was really his wife. She only got stolen moments of his time, and he'd almost seemed guilty about the time he'd spent with her, the time away from his job. It hadn't been fair to Valentina. She shouldn't have been alone so much while he'd been working nights and weekends in addition to all week long. She'd deserved so much more from their marriage, from him. She'd deserved everything she'd wanted.

She was so sweet and loving and smart and beautiful. So very beautiful…

He could see her now in his mind, and maybe he even conjured up her image through the side window. Her thick dark hair flowing nearly to her waist, her hips swaying as she walked along the sidewalk. But she was pushing something in front of her. A stroller?

Was she babysitting for a friend?

Or had she started that family, the one she'd wanted with him, with someone else? That was what he'd hoped for her when he'd divorced her, but knowing that she had actually moved on with someone else...

And he hadn't. He was still stuck in their past, dreaming of her smile, of her laugh, of her wicked sense of humor flashing in her dark eyes, and the love...

A car horn tooted behind him and he realized the light had changed to green and the traffic in front of him had moved. But he was still stuck...

He pressed on the accelerator and surged forward through the intersection. The light green at the next one, he drove through that as well because he spied an open parking space ahead on the curb. He was nearly to her condo building. That had to be where she was heading. So he pulled into that spot and hopped out of his SUV. She would be coming this way if she was going home.

But maybe she'd been babysitting for someone and was taking the child back to their parents. Or was she the parent? Had she had the child she wanted? The family?

He wanted to be happy for her. But a part of him had never stopped wanting her. And if that was her he'd seen on the sidewalk, she was every bit as beautiful as she'd always been. As sexy...

His heart pounded hard as he skirted his SUV and stepped onto the sidewalk. He'd gotten only a couple of blocks ahead of her. She should appear soon, but the sidewalk was packed with people heading toward him, probably intent on enjoying the sunny day at the amusement park or the beach. And her complex was so close to both.

Instead of waiting for her to pass by him, Cash started through the crowd, moving against the throng of people. It had been three years since he'd seen Valentina; maybe that hadn't even been her he'd glimpsed on the sidewalk. Maybe that woman just looked like Valentina with the same curves and the same walk.

But if that woman wasn't his ex-wife, he doubted his heart would be pounding as fast and hard as it was. It wasn't just attraction or anticipation coursing through him, though; it was fear. Something had compelled him to drive out to Coney Island today to make sure she was safe. He'd been worried since he'd received that text, but that worry had intensified, twisting his guts, because he had a sick feeling, almost a premonition, that she was in danger.

He moved faster through the crowd, drawing grunts and curses as he accidentally banged into people. Maybe if they hadn't been on their phones and distracted, they would have seen him coming, but he grunted back apologies. Until he neared the next intersection and he saw *her* standing on the other side; then he was the one distracted.

The woman was definitely Valentina. She stood at the curb, in front of that stroller although she was half-turned toward it, her hand on the top of it as if she was protecting it from the traffic on the street in front of her. The breeze coming in off the ocean played with her hair, swirling the long chocolate-brown tresses around her, while it plastered her light blue cotton dress against her curves. He knew that body so well that his tightened with the desire coursing through him. He'd never wanted anyone the way he'd wanted her.

The way he still wanted her…

She didn't see him. Her focus was split between that stroller and the crosswalk light. Once it turned green, she held back a moment, letting other people pass by her. Then, finally, she started across, and just as she did, Cash heard an engine rev, brakes squeal and metal scrape as a car sideswiped the one stopped in front of it to pass it and roar toward the intersection, toward Valentina and that stroller with not one but two children in it.

His heart slammed against his ribs as fear shot through him. He'd been right to worry about her; she was definitely in danger.

Mortal danger…

The asphalt was hard and hot beneath her back. The impact with which Valentina had struck the ground had knocked the breath from her lungs, and she couldn't get it back, not with the heavy weight lying on top of her, pressing her into the ground. Panic gripped her, and now her lungs burned with a scream as well as lack of breath.

The kids!

The stroller. Had it been knocked over as well? Or had the car done that?

It wasn't the car lying atop Valentina; it was a long,

hard body. A familiar body even now, after three years; she recognized the feel of it pressed against hers. Instead of savoring the sensation, Valentina shoved at his shoulders, pushing him off. She had to find her babies.

Their babies…

The stroller was still upright, but the girls were crying and reaching out toward her. Fortunately they were strapped in yet, and while they were scared, they didn't appear harmed. Tears streaked out of Valentina's eyes.

Cash, who'd rolled off her, vaulted to his feet and helped her up. "Are you all right?"

She didn't care about herself; she ran toward her children, checking on them. Making sure they were okay. No scratches. No bumps or bruises. So, thank God, the car hadn't struck the stroller at all. Cash must have shoved it out of the way when he'd knocked her down.

"It's okay, it's okay," she murmured to them. Then she turned back toward Cash and asked, "What happened?"

"A black Ford Taurus nearly ran us down," Cash said, but he was speaking into his cell phone, reciting a plate number that he must have somehow been able to read. He wasn't even looking at her. Or the kids.

She didn't want him to; she didn't want him to see her and definitely didn't want him to get a good look at the girls. Most of all, she didn't want to have to explain what she'd done and why she'd kept the secret for so long.

Right now she just wanted to get herself and her daughters safely away from there, far from that car and even farther from Cash.

But as she reached for the handle of the stroller, she heard the deep rev of an engine again and the squeal of tires. And she turned and saw that the black car had started back toward them…

Damn it!

How the hell had he missed?

He'd been so close. Too close to give up so soon. No matter how many people had called 9-1-1, the police wouldn't get there for a few minutes. So he turned around at the next intersection, scraping cars that were parked along the curb as he made that sharp U-turn so that once again he was facing that intersection.

The woman was standing again, right in the middle of the street, next to that big stroller.

Totally focused on his target, he pressed hard on the accelerator and headed straight toward them.

This time he would not miss.

Chapter 3

Cash dived for Valentina and the stroller again, shoving them out of the way even as he drew his weapon and aimed at the vehicle, at the person in the driver's seat, his hands gripping the steering wheel. The person wore a mask, and his hood was pulled tight around his face.

It had to be…

The Landmark Killer.

Cash stared down the barrel of his gun at the masked driver, but then he aimed for the tires and squeezed the trigger. One tire blew and another, but the car continued on, turning sharply with a squeal of rubber slapping against asphalt and another screech of metal as it scraped another car.

Then it sped away, sparks flying from the rims hitting the road.

Even though he'd shot out two of the tires, he couldn't be certain that it wouldn't come back, that it wouldn't try for them again. And the driver was probably armed, too.

Some of the Landmark Killer's victims had been shot.

None of them had been run down.

And none had been women or children. But the killer wasn't really after them; he was probably only trying to send Cash a message.

People were in danger because of him, because of their special unit's determination to catch and stop the serial killer. And if they stayed on this busy street, more innocent people might get hurt because of him.

"We have to get out of here," he told Valentina. Checking to make sure the black car was gone, he holstered his weapon and reached for the stroller. Instead of pushing it, he picked it up and rushed down the sidewalk toward her building.

Valentina kept pace with him, running either from danger or to stop him from rushing off with the kids, who cried as he carried them.

They had to be terrified, like Valentina obviously was. Her dark eyes were wide with fear and shock. "This way," she said, her voice shaking as she started across the street.

But Cash caught her arm, holding her back, making sure that neither the black Ford nor any other vehicle was careening toward her. When he saw a break in the traffic, he hurried across with her and that stroller.

Once across the street, she ran for a gate, punching in the code so that it opened to a parking lot and the high-rise building beyond it. Then she released a shaky breath as if they were safe. Cash wasn't as convinced. Since the Landmark Killer could send an untraceable text and know so much about him and his siblings, the smart psychopath could probably figure out the code to that gate as well.

They weren't safe just because the gate closed behind them. It could open again. It could let the killer back inside. So Cash didn't slow down and didn't let her slow down, either, until they were inside, up the elevator, down the hall and locked inside her condo.

Then finally he released a ragged breath of relief and his tight grip on the stroller, settling it onto the floor in the narrow foyer.

"It's okay, it's okay," Valentina said, repeating what she'd been telling the kids since the car had nearly run them down. She knelt in front of the stroller and unclipped the belts securing them into their seats. Then she pulled them into her arms, hugging their small, trembling bodies close against her. They were the same height so probably the same age. They were somewhere in that toddler range. Twins? "You're safe now, my babies. We're home."

"Home?" His voice cracked on the word.

They were home? They lived here…with her? But as he noticed the finger-painted and crayon artwork framed and hanging on the foyer walls as well as pictures of them at all different stages of their lives, he realized that they did live here.

With Valentina…

They were hers.

Their hair was a little lighter brown, though, and curly, like his if he didn't get it cut often enough. Then one of the little girls raised her head from Valentina's shoulder and stared up at him with green eyes the exact same shade as his. And his heart contracted as it had when he'd seen that car heading toward Valentina and that stroller.

Were they his, too?

Despite being home, in the place where she'd always felt the safest and happiest, Valentina was scared and on edge. The door was locked. And with their being on the eleventh floor, there was no way a car could come up here and ram into it, like it had tried ramming into them on the street. Not once but twice…

She trembled as she thought of it, of the close call she and the girls had had, but she forced a smile for her daughters. The car was no longer a threat, but Cash was.

He was still here. And she was tense, on edge, because she knew what was to come. Cash had only had a chance to ask Valentina one question, if his just repeating the word *home* in that strangled-sounding voice had actually been a question, before his cell had rung and vibrated loudly in his pocket. With its persistent ringing, he'd had to pick it up. He'd been on his phone ever since, explaining why he'd chosen to leave the scene instead of waiting for the local police to arrive.

To protect them and to protect the other people on the street. With the way the car had kept coming at them, the driver had been so determined that he might have tried again even after Cash had taken those shots at the tires.

Who was the driver? The person who'd sent Cash that text about her?

Her ex-husband hadn't even told her what it had said specifically, just that it had mentioned her and that made him uneasy. He'd warned her that the killer was very dangerous, and she needed to be alert and aware of the potential threat.

But she hadn't been alert and aware since that call, or at least not enough. She'd been distracted, and if he hadn't showed up when he had today…

She shuddered again, thinking of what could have happened to her daughters. To their daughters.

She struggled to comfort them now. They were clinging to her yet, trembling within her embrace. Or maybe she was the one shaking with fear in reaction to what had happened and over what could still happen when Cash realized what she'd done.

The secret she'd kept.

The secrets…

Luci and Ana.

"Mommy…" Ana whispered, her usually soft voice a little raspy from all the crying she'd done.

"Who that man?" she asked, pointing one small hand toward Cash, where he paced in front of the windows, his cell phone pressed to his ear instead of on speaker.

He probably didn't want them to overhear the other side of his conversation. Was he getting yelled at for leaving the scene?

She was grateful that he'd picked up the stroller, that he'd whisked the twins away from the chaos and danger. They'd been scared when he'd picked up the stroller and run with it, but they probably hadn't realized he'd been protecting them. Were they even aware of what had happened? How much danger they'd been in?

Not yet three years old, they were so young, but they were smart and observant, too. And they'd known enough to be afraid when that car had nearly run them down, or as empathetic as they were, maybe they'd just felt her fear.

That fear hadn't left her yet. She'd never been so scared in that moment when she'd been knocked to the ground and she hadn't known what had happened to the stroller, to the girls.

Her heart ached with that fear, and her arms were starting to ache, too, from holding them so close.

Luci wriggled away from her now and turned around to face her. "Who that man?" she repeated her twin's question, as if Valentina hadn't understood Ana and she'd needed to translate for her sister as she often did.

Valentina understood. She just wasn't certain how to answer it. With the truth…

Or…

"He's an FBI agent," she answered with the most information that she cared to reveal right now and in order to soothe their concerns about him. His having the gun and firing it at the car had probably scared them into thinking he was a bad man, and then he'd picked up the stroller, probably scaring them even more and making them worry that he might hurt them.

She was more worried about his hurting her for keeping them secret from him. He wouldn't physically hurt her; Cash was too gentle a man for that. But he had every right to be furious with her.

"What?" Ana asked.

"What fib?" Luci added her question.

Their little brows creased beneath the fall of their curls. Clearly they didn't understand what an FBI agent was.

"An FBI agent is like a policeman," she explained. "He's a good guy." And he really was. He deserved to have known the truth, that he'd become a father.

But that was a responsibility he'd never wanted to have, not when he already shouldered more than he could physically handle with his job on that serial killer task force. So when she'd finally figured out she was pregnant, after the divorce papers had already been signed and filed, she hadn't wanted to saddle him with more responsibility, especially one he hadn't wanted.

But she was honest enough with herself to admit she'd acted selfishly, too. She'd known the only way she would ever get over losing him was to have no further contact with him. But as she stared at him now, looking so handsome and serious, his brow creased like his daughters' as he listened to his caller, she knew it hadn't worked. Her heart reacted the way it always had to him, beating faster, fluttering in her chest.

His hair was getting long enough that it was starting to curl, and his beard was longer than he usually had it. But she'd never minded if he hadn't trimmed it. It was soft, and she'd loved it brushing across her face when they'd kissed as well as the other parts of her body that he'd kissed. He'd always been such a thorough lover. She'd never even tried to be with anyone else since the divorce.

She'd told herself that it was because of the girls, because they needed all her time and attention. But it was really because she'd known no other man would compare to Cash Colton.

Despite not seeing him for three years, she wasn't really over him.

She wondered if she would ever be…

Ashlynn Colton had been so afraid when she'd gotten that call from her brother Cash. As an FBI special agent, he was often in danger; she knew that. But one of her other brothers, Cash's twin Brennan, had recently had some close calls, too. And knowing she could have lost him, like they'd lost their dad, had had them all on edge.

Then Cash had received the next text after Brennan received his. Their cousin Sinead, the FBI profiler, had gotten the first one. But no matter how hard Ashlynn had tried, she'd been unable to trace any of them. They were sent from burner phones and rerouted through ISPs so they bounced off so many towers that she couldn't even pinpoint a location.

New York.

She knew that. It had to be. But she hadn't been able to figure out any more. Frustration gnawed at her over that; she was an FBI tech expert. She should have been able to find out more about the phones, about who'd purchased them.

Should have been able to track down the sender of those damned texts. And maybe if she had, Cash wouldn't have been in the danger he'd been in just a short time ago.

He'd called her from the scene, firing off that plate number to her, but then she'd heard an engine revving and the squeal of tires on asphalt, and she knew the vehicle had returned, the driver coming back after Cash.

Her brother had cursed and disconnected the call. And she'd spent a long while wondering what had happened even as she'd called 9-1-1 for him. Even as she'd run the plate number he'd given her...

"That car was just reported stolen twenty minutes ago," she said now.

The owner had been shopping on Coney Island

and had worried that they'd forgotten where they'd
parked. But they hadn't been able to find it anywhere
until they'd witnessed it careening down the street
toward a young family. That was what they'd said
in the 9-1-1 call Ashlynn had "borrowed" from the
Coney Island emergency services department.

"Cash?" she asked. "What the hell happened?"

"I told you," he said. "That vehicle tried running
us down."

"Who's us, Cash?" she asked, but she had a feeling she knew at least part of it. But family...what
did that mean?

Predictably he replied, "Valentina..."

But a man and a woman would have been called
a couple, not a family. "And?" she prodded. She
could tell there was more, and not just because of
that 9-1-1 tape she'd heard and the police report she'd
read about the stolen vehicle, but because she knew
her brother.

He sounded distracted and upset, and Cash wasn't
easily rattled. That text had rattled him, though. He'd
never gotten over his ex-wife. None of them really
had; Valentina Acosta was so fun and sweet and so
good for Cash, who'd tended to work too much and
take on way too much responsibility.

Ashlynn wasn't certain why Valentina and Cash
had gotten divorced. They'd seemed crazy about
each other; they'd had the kind of relationship other
people envied. The way they'd looked at each other,
the love that had radiated out of their eyes. She'd en-

vied their relationship, but she could also understand why it might not have lasted.

She and all her siblings had a tendency to let the job consume them. Because of how they'd lost their dad, they understood all too well how hard it was to lose someone you loved to a serial killer in a senseless act of violence that had nothing to do with the victim.

Except wrong place, wrong time…

Was that the case with Cash, though? Or was the Landmark Killer stalking him now even though Cash certainly didn't match the profile of the other victims?

While the Landmark Killer had sent Brennan and Sinead texts, he hadn't made attempts on their lives. Why Cash and Valentina?

"Cash?" She prodded him again when she realized he hadn't answered her yet. "Who else was there besides you and Valentina?"

"Her daughters," he mumbled into the phone.

"Her daughters?" Ashlynn repeated. "Valentina has a couple of kids?"

"Twins," he murmured faintly.

Like him and Brennan. She wanted to ask more, but before she could fire her questions at him, he said, "I have another call coming in, Ashlynn. I need to go."

She hadn't heard anything on the line to indicate that he was telling the truth. She suspected he had another reason for ending the call. He didn't want to give her a chance to ask any more questions about Valentina and her twin daughters.

Why?

Because the answers were too painful for him or because he didn't know them?

"Cash, please be careful," she said. But she was too late. Her brother had already hung up.

He hadn't heard her warning, but she didn't know if he would have heeded it even if he had. Cash had already been intent, as they all were, on catching the Landmark Killer, long before he'd sent that text about Valentina.

Now…

If it had been the Landmark Killer driving the stolen car, then Cash was undoubtedly even more determined. But at what risk and what cost?

The same one their father had paid?

With his life?

Chapter 4

Cash hadn't had another call. But he'd known where the conversation with his sister was heading, to questions he couldn't answer until he'd asked them himself.

But even though another call hadn't been coming in, a knock had come at the door. And, just like Ashlynn, he hadn't had the chance to ask the questions he needed the answers for, of the only person who could really answer them: Valentina.

He wound up answering questions, though, when he opened the door to an officer from the local precinct, the one he'd asked to periodically check on Valentina. This wasn't the officer he'd asked, though; this guy was older than Dave. Probably closer to retirement, whereas Dave Percell was just a couple years older than Cash. Why hadn't Sergeant Dave Percell warned him about the twins? If he'd been watching out for her like Cash asked him to, then Dave had to realize that they were with her all the time so they were hers. That she wasn't the only one in danger because of him.

But he saved those questions while he answered this older officer's questions about what had happened in the street, with the stolen car. He wished Dave had come instead to take the report, but he was off for the day, which was why Cash had felt compelled to check on Valentina himself.

That and he'd just wanted to see her for himself, to make sure she was really okay since he'd had that nagging feeling in his gut that she wasn't. And he'd been right.

He didn't explain all that to this officer, though. Just kept everything quick and impersonal. Or as quick as he could, given that the officer asked Valentina all the same questions he had Cash and then he crouched down to fire those same questions at the kids.

Dave might have done a better job getting the kids to talk since he had five of his own. Cash had known the man a long time; they'd both been up for the same job with the FBI. But Cash had beat him out for it, which Dave had repeatedly assured him was a blessing because he wouldn't have had time for his family if he'd had Cash's job. A family obligation was why he was off today, leaving this loud, awkward officer to take the report.

But the girls were shy. They ducked behind their mother and refused to answer any of the officer's questions. Cash had heard them talking to Valentina while he'd been on the phone with his sister. They'd asked about him. They didn't know who or what he was. And at the moment neither did Cash for certain; he just had his suspicion.

The older officer focused on Cash again. Obviously he knew what case he was working on, maybe because of that damn article in the *New York Wire* or maybe Dave Percell had let him know. The guy asked, "So you think it could be the Landmark..." He trailed off with a glance at the girls and Valentina.

"I'll take them into their room now," she said, probably anxious to get them away from that conversation. Or away from Cash?

But before he could let them go, Cash had to ask, "You're sure they weren't harmed?"

She nodded. "The stroller never tipped over. They're fine. Just scared." Like she clearly still was.

Like Cash was...

"And you?" Cash asked.

He should have asked her that earlier, after he'd pushed her out of the way of the vehicle and they'd hit the asphalt. But she'd gotten right up; she'd run to the stroller. She'd run to her building, keeping up with him as he carried the stroller. So he'd assumed she was fine, and he really hadn't had a chance to ask her before now.

But he could see how mussed her long hair was, and the torn material of one dress sleeve revealed a scrape on her skin. He must have done that when he'd knocked her to the ground.

"Did you get hurt when I pushed you down?" he asked her, his voice gruff with concern and guilt. He hadn't just pushed her; he'd pretty much tackled her.

She shook her head. "No. I'm fine. Really." But her voice had cracked as she made the claim.

And he knew she wasn't fine at all. But before he could challenge her assertion, she turned away from him and the officer and, holding one of the hands of each of the twins, she steered the children through the living room to the short hallway off it.

She'd changed the condo a lot since he'd visited her grandparents with her more than three years ago. Their cold red leather couch had been replaced with a soft, brushed-looking suede sectional, and the glass coffee table was gone, replaced by a brightly patterned cloth ottoman.

Everything about the place looked brighter and warmer and softer...even Valentina, except when she looked at him. If she looked at him...

She didn't even spare him a backward glance as she disappeared through the doorway off the living room.

"So you think it's the Landmark Killer?" Officer Hooper finished the question he'd been asking before Valentina had whisked away the twins.

Cash tensed with fear and dread about the danger his ex-wife and her daughters were in because of him. Because of his job. And were Valentina's daughters his? They looked to be around two or three, not that he was an expert on kids, but that was the age they would be if she'd been pregnant when she left him.

He had to ask her. Had to know…

But right now he needed to focus on how much danger they were in.

"I don't know if it's him," he answered the officer. "We only have a vague description of the Landmark Killer, and with the driver wearing a mask and a hoodie—" which was part of that vague but also very common description of the serial killer "—I can't tell you much about his appearance."

And now that he knew the car had been stolen, it was just another dead end leading to nowhere.

The best lead the FBI special unit had to the killer was the texts he'd sent to taunt them. Because of everything he knew about them personally, they all had realized that he had to be close to them somehow and maybe he was also in law enforcement.

Cash could really only trust his family and a few other select individuals who were either becoming part of the family or had been friends for many years. Like Dave Percell. But maybe it was good that Dave had been off today and out of the area, or Cash might not have been so compelled to check on Valentina himself. He might have sent his friend instead, to make sure she was safe.

She wasn't, and neither were her daughters. He really had to know if they were his, too. And if they were, why she hadn't told him…

"A few other officers stayed behind at the scene to interview pedestrians and shop owners and street vendors who might have seen something, too," Officer Hooper said. "Hopefully they'll come up with something more to go on than…"

A stolen car and a description that could have been anyone wearing that disguise. A man or a woman, young or old. It wasn't enough to prove to the local authorities or to Cash that it had been the Landmark Killer behind the steering wheel. But whoever it was, the person had been so intent on killing that they'd turned around and tried again.

And would they keep trying?

"Will you be staying here?" the officer asked. He'd probably noted that for the report Cash had given a different address for his home than this condo. Though his last name and Valentina's were still the same. Even after the divorce, she'd kept Colton. Was that the girls' last name, too?

He had to talk to her, his gut as tight with dread as it had been when he'd sensed that she was in danger. "I'll let you know," he told the officer as he walked him out the door. As he closed it behind him, his cell vibrated with another call. The sergeant from the local precinct that Cash fully trusted.

"Hey, Dave," he answered.

"I heard about what happened," Dave Percell said. "Sorry I wasn't in the area today."

"How many people knew that?" Cash wondered.

"That I had an appointment in the city?" Dave asked. "A lot of people in my precinct."

So there could be someone even here who could be working with the killer or could be the killer. Maybe that was how he'd known Valentina was sad.

But was she?

She'd been scared, rightfully so, over that car trying to run down her and her daughters. But sad…

"I'm back in Coney Island now," the guy continued. "I can come by…"

"The condo," Cash said. "As soon as you can." Cash had some things he needed to do, but he didn't want to leave Valentina and the girls alone again.

The first thing he needed to do, though, before anything else, was to figure out the truth. Once Dave assured him that he was on his way, Cash disconnected the call and went to find Valentina.

She sat on the floor in a narrow space between two twin beds. Each bed had a curly-haired twin tucked under a bright pink fleece blanket. The walls were a pale pink, almost blush color, while the curtains were bright pink like the blankets. One girl had a purple teddy bear clasped in her arms, the other a stuffed white bunny.

As Valentina read from a book she held up between them, their eyelids began to droop, falling down over first the set of dark eyes that looked so much like her mother's, and then the others over the green eyes that looked so much like Cash's.

Their little bodies slumped and relaxed, and soft snoring emanated from first one and then the other. And some of the tension eased from his body that they felt safe now.

"They're asleep," he whispered to Valentina who'd continued to read.

She'd probably realized they were out but hadn't

wanted to stop reading because she suspected what he was going to ask her. What he had to know…

He waited until she got up from the floor and joined him in the hall, closing the bedroom door behind her, before he asked, "Are they mine?"

She sucked in a breath and stepped around him, walking into the living room. Maybe she hadn't wanted their conversation to wake the twins. Or maybe she was worried about how he was going to react. Or maybe she just had no intention of answering him and that was why she'd walked away from him.

He followed her to where she stood before the windows that looked out onto Coney Island. The myriad lights of the rides at Luna Park sparkled down below. The condo building was close to the amusement park and to the water that glistened beyond the rides, its surface reflecting the last pinkish glow of the sun that must have just set. Days were already starting to get shorter now that summer was slipping away in September.

"Valentina?" he prodded her.

She stood in front of those tall windows, her arms wrapped around herself as if she was cold or, more likely, scared. Of what had happened? Or of his reaction to what she'd clearly kept from him?

His children.

"Are they mine?" he asked again.

As if preparing herself for a fight, she drew in another breath and straightened her shoulders before she turned around to face him. Then she quietly replied, "Yes."

And Cash wished he'd prepared himself for her response, because he felt like he had when that car had come at them. Stunned. Scared. But this time, instead of getting out of the way, he'd let it run him down. The wind was knocked out of him and his heart pounded furiously and for a moment he couldn't breathe, couldn't even think, as if he was in shock.

And, despite the suspicion he'd had when he'd seen the one little girl's eyes, he *was* shocked. He was shocked that he was a father. And he was even more shocked that Valentina had never told him he was.

Her heart hammering in her chest, Valentina waited for him to yell at her. She'd braced herself for him to react that way with the breath she'd drawn in, the one that burned now in her lungs. She released it in a ragged sigh as she continued to wait for him to do something. Anything…

But he just stood there, the exact same way she'd stood in the street as that car had barreled toward her and the stroller. She hadn't done anything then; she'd been too frozen with fear and shock to react.

Was that Cash's issue?

Realizing that she hadn't expressed her gratitude yet for his saving her and their daughters, she murmured, "Thank you."

He tensed then and stared at her, his green eyes wide with that shock he was obviously reeling from. "Are you thanking me for them?"

"I'm thanking you for saving them," she explained. "And me from that car. That was…that could have…" She could have lost their daughters and her own life if he hadn't been there, if he hadn't reacted as quickly as he had then. Maybe that was why she found it so unnerving that he hadn't reacted now, to her admission that the girls were his, too.

"It's probably my fault that you're in danger," he said. "That text…"

"Did it specifically threaten me? Us?" she asked.

When he'd called her a week ago to tell her about it, she hadn't asked any questions because she'd been anxious to get him off the phone before he overheard the girls chattering in the background. She hadn't wanted him to ask about them like he just had.

He shook his head. "It didn't mention *them* at all. Just my ex-wife…"

She narrowed her eyes, suspecting there was more. Something he'd left out. "What about me?" She should have asked that a week ago; she probably should have asked to see the text since it had mentioned her. Then she might not have been so shocked today. "Tell me what it said."

He hesitated.

"I have a right to know," she pointed out. "Since it mentions me."

"I had a right to know about them," he replied, his voice gruff with anger.

And she flinched, but she couldn't argue with him. He had had a right to know, and she had struggled with guilt all these years over keeping them secret. "Yes, you did," she conceded.

"Why didn't you tell me?" he asked.

She flinched again and reminded him, "Because you didn't want them."

"I didn't know—"

"You didn't want to be a father," she said. "You made that very clear to me." He hadn't done that until she'd told him she wanted to start their family. With as much as they'd worked, and all the passion between them when he was home, the conversation that they should have had before they got married hadn't happened until it was too late.

He didn't argue with her now, just sucked in a breath as if she'd struck him.

"And when you had your lawyer serve me with divorce papers, you made it very clear that you didn't want to be a husband, either." She wondered then as she had over the course of their three-year marriage and the three years since they'd divorced why he'd proposed, why he'd married her at all, if he'd never wanted the same things she had.

If he'd never really wanted her...

The minute she'd moved out to clear her head, to think about what compromise could work for both of them, he'd served her...as if he'd wanted to make sure that she wouldn't try to come home again.

But she'd been home the minute she'd moved into the condo on Coney Island that she'd loved so much. But not as much as she'd once loved him.

"All you wanted was your job," she pointed out.

Finally he moved then, stepping closer to her, so close that she could feel the heat and tension in his long, lean body. His body was so hard, so muscular that he'd always made her feel so soft and feminine, so sexy, especially when he looked at her like was looking at her now, with all that heat and desire in his green eyes.

"That's not true," he said. "I did want you, all the time."

She closed her eyes as memories rolled through her mind, of his kisses, his caresses, of the passion that had burned so hotly between them. But maybe it had been too hot, and that was why it had burned out so quickly.

Or had it?

She felt the attraction to him that she always had, the tingling in her skin, the rapid beat of her pulse, but maybe that was just fear over what had happened and over what he would do now that he knew the truth.

About their girls...

"I'm staying," he said.

She opened her eyes and stared up at him in surprise. "What?"

"I need to get some things from my place first, but I have a friend from the local precinct coming by to stand guard in the hall until I get back. Dave Percell. Do you remember him?"

She shook her head. She hadn't met many of his work friends. When he hadn't been working, they spent all their time together or with their families.

"But I am coming back, Valentina," he told her.

"You..." She shook her head. "You can't." She wouldn't feel safe with him staying here with her and the girls. She wouldn't feel safe not because she was afraid of what he might do or expect but because of what *she* might do or expect. Like for him to stay…

And it would be even worse if the girls expected that, too, because they would get as disappointed and heartbroken as she'd been.

"You and…" His voice trailed off as his throat moved as if he was choking on something, then he continued. "Our daughters might be in danger because of me. I'm going to stay here to protect you all until this sociopath is caught."

She shook her head. "That's not necessary. We'll be fine without…"

"Without me?" he finished for her. "I guess you were fine the past three years."

But she hadn't been fine without him. Not really. And especially not today. In fact without him, she and the girls might have been killed.

"I see that you've managed just fine," he said. "But this is different. This is real danger. Surely you had to realize how close a call you had today, that you all had today?"

She shivered and nodded. "Too close."

If he hadn't been there…

She couldn't think of what might have happened to their daughters. To her…

"I just don't understand why this killer would come after me," she said. It wasn't as if Cash was still in love with her, if he'd ever been in love with her. Because if he had, wouldn't they have been able to find a compromise, a way to stay together that would have made them both happy?

He pulled out his cell phone then and pulled up a text that he showed her.

The text...

She skimmed over the line about the actor and read the last part. Tsk-tsk, Cash—murdered daddy and a sad ex-wife.

She bristled with indignation and wanted to deny this sick killer's claim. She wasn't sad. She had her daughters who made every day, every moment, special. A job she enjoyed. A home she loved. And friends...

But she didn't have Cash.

She never really had, though. Because even though they'd shared a bed for three years, he'd never really shared his life with her.

Another text came into his phone. I'm here.

And she let out a little gasp, wondering if that was from the killer as well.

But Cash headed toward the door. "Dave's here. I'll have him stand guard outside the door. He'll protect you and the girls until I get back."

Who would protect her then, once he returned? Who would protect her from falling for him all over again?

Before bullets had taken out two of the car tires, the gun had been aimed right at him, and if it had fired then, it could have struck him right in the face. In the mask...

He was so damn glad he'd put the mask on after he'd stolen that car. If only he'd been wearing it earlier, when he'd killed...

But it was too late to undo what had already been done. All he could do was try to fix it now. Like he'd tried to fix it by running them all down.

But that hadn't worked. He stared at the car, that sat lopsided with the two flat tires, in an empty parking lot. He was lucky that he'd managed to keep driving, to get away. He'd had a close escape.

Too close.

He had to be more careful next time. Had to make damn sure that he didn't miss, with the car, or with whatever weapon he chose next.

He had to get rid of this weapon: the car, which had proven ineffective. He had to make sure that there was nothing left inside it that could be traced back to him.

So he dragged in a deep breath of gasoline fumes from the liquid he'd poured all over the seats. The acrid scent burned his nose and throat, making him cough and sputter. He glanced around to make sure nobody lurked in the shadows, in the dark.

Then he lit a match, striking it to a wad of cloth, and tossed it inside that car, onto the seat. And with a whoosh of air, flames sprang up, burning the upholstery, burning his DNA…

Taking away every trace of him inside that vehicle. But he wasn't done yet. He couldn't leave until he'd accomplished everything he'd promised to do.

Chapter 5

Cash pushed open the door to his apartment to a rush of stale air. He didn't even remember the last time he'd been here. He'd been staying mostly at the office, using the locker room to shower and wearing the clothes he'd stashed in his locker. He'd run out of clean ones, though.

That was why he'd left the office today. To clean up and grab some fresh clothes. But he'd figured, with Dave not working today, that he should drive out to Coney Island first and make sure that Valentina was okay. Especially with that gut feeling nagging at him.

He'd also wanted to find out if she really was sad. He thought of how she'd looked standing at that curb, waiting for the light to change. She hadn't looked sad to him. Beautiful. So damn beautiful…

And distracted maybe…like he was whenever he thought of her.

With being a single working mother, she had every reason to be distracted and stressed and tired.

She was single, wasn't she?

He'd never asked. He'd just assumed, and when he'd told her that he was staying at her place, she hadn't told him that he couldn't because she had a partner. Not that he was staying with her in that capacity.

Clearly he'd never really been a partner to her, and all he could offer her right now was protection. Because she wasn't wrong. He hadn't really wanted to be a husband or a father. And if he hadn't fallen so damn fast and so damn hard for her, he wouldn't have even tried to change his mind, to change the plan he'd always had for his future. To catch and stop as many serial killers as he and his team could.

But once he'd met her, at a library in the city, he hadn't been able to imagine his future without her in it. But she'd wanted a future he hadn't been willing to give her.

She had it now. She had the children she'd wanted. She lived where she'd wanted them to move, into the condo where she'd made a warm and comfortable home for her and the girls.

So he should be happy for her. He shouldn't be sad, and he shouldn't be angry and resentful, which was how he felt now, which was what churned inside his empty stomach. He wasn't going to take the time to eat now; maybe he would pick up something on the way back to Valentina's. The pizza she'd always loved from the place down the street.

Unless they'd eaten before he'd seen them walking back to the condo, she had probably not eaten, either. The girls hadn't.

But they must have been so exhausted over their ordeal that they'd fallen asleep without thinking about it. Hopefully they wouldn't think about what happened; they wouldn't have nightmares about it.

He suspected he would, that he would keep seeing that car aiming for them, the driver hell-bent on hurting them or worse. Killing them…

Why?

They certainly were not at all remotely similar to the Landmark Killer's other victims, who'd all been male, as the victims of Maeve O'Leary, the Black Widow, had been. She'd tried to kill a woman, too, though. And since the Landmark Killer obviously idolized her, was that why he'd made this attempt on Valentina's life?

Or hadn't it been him at all?

Cash really didn't know anything about Valentina anymore, if he ever had. He'd always thought she was so straightforward and honest, but she'd kept a life-changing secret from him for three years.

She'd kept his children from him for three years. That anger surged through him again, and he hurriedly packed up some clothes and toiletries into a duffel bag. With its handle clutched tightly in his hand, he stepped out his door, locked it behind him and headed down the stairwell at the end of the hall to the parking garage in the basement.

As he started toward where he'd parked the SUV, he heard a door open and close behind him. Had someone else been in the stairwell?

It hadn't been a car door he'd heard; it had been heavier, like the steel door to the stairs. It could have just been another resident leaving when he was, but when he turned back, he noticed no one walking behind him. Nothing but shadows in the dimly lit concrete structure.

He turned back and continued walking to where he'd parked the FBI SUV, but then he heard the scrape of shoe soles against the concrete. And he knew for certain that he was not alone.

Someone else was inside the parking garage. Someone who clearly didn't want to be seen.

Cash carefully reached inside his jacket for his holster, pulling out the weapon he'd fired already once that day, and he was prepared to fire again.

To do whatever necessary to get back to his family...

Family.

For so long after his dad's death, that had been just his mom and siblings. That was the only family he'd ever intended to have, so that he didn't leave anyone behind mourning him like they'd all mourned his dad.

The footsteps hastened behind him and he whirled around with his weapon. He wasn't going down without one hell of a fight.

* * *

The girls had been fighting so hard to stay awake earlier, but once Valentina had started reading to them, it had been clear how exhausted they'd been from their long day and from that scare with the car and with Cash.

He had frightened them when he'd picked up their stroller and run with it like he'd had earlier. But he'd only been trying to keep them safe. To protect them.

And he intended to move in to do that, to keep them safe. She believed that was his only intention, or she would have definitely refused. But after what had happened, how the car had turned around and come back, she couldn't deny that they were in danger.

From whom?

A serial killer?

Was that who had really been driving that car?

But why come after her and the kids?

Cash's sad ex-wife…

She shivered as she realized this person must have been watching her. Following her…

Why not mention the children to Cash? Because there was no doubt he'd been shocked to learn about them. Maybe that was what the texter had intended, though. For Cash to seek her out and find out the secret she'd been keeping from him.

Was this all some sick joke this person was pulling? Manipulating Cash into contacting her again, into finding out the truth? To hurt him? To rattle him? To distract him from his quest for justice?

She hated that she and her children had become

pawns in this game a killer was playing with Cash and his team. That article in the *New York Wire* had mentioned every member of the FBI's special serial killer unit as well as dredging up what had happened to Cash's father.

Murdered daddy...

Sympathy flooded her heart for Cash and his siblings and for her daughters as well. They'd lost their grandfather without ever getting the chance to know him because of a killer. She was the one who'd denied the rest of them knowing the girls.

She felt almost guiltier about that than she did about keeping them from Cash. His mother would have loved spoiling her granddaughters, might even have moved home from Florida where she'd relocated after retiring. And Brennan and Patrick would have struggled to relate to the girls, probably like their father would have, but they would have made the effort because family mattered to them.

And Ashlynn...

Valentina smiled as she thought of the brilliant young woman she'd been fortunate to call her sister for three years. She'd missed Ashlynn the most of her in-laws because she'd always wanted a sister.

But Valentina had known that in order to get over Cash, she'd had to make a clean break from all the Coltons. She hadn't known then that she was already pregnant with two more of them.

And now a killer was after all the Coltons on that special serial killer unit and maybe Valentina as well. And even her daughters?

A cry broke the silence in the condo, startling Valentina into releasing one of her own. She ran to the bedroom, desperate to make sure the girls were okay. When she opened the door, she found Luci wrapping her arms around Ana, as if trying to comfort her as Ana cried, tears streaking down her face.

"What's wrong?" Valentina asked with concern. They'd been through too much today.

Ana pulled away from her sister to raise her hand and point. "Bad...bad..."

"Just a bad dream?" Valentina asked.

Ana shook her head. "No. Bad man..."

Valentina glanced around the room, but there was no monster hiding in the shadows. Just their dollhouse and toys.

But she shouldn't have expected to see anything else. The only way in or out of the condo was through the door that one of Cash's friends and colleagues guarded.

They had to be safe.

Now.

For the moment.

She crossed the room to join the two of them in Ana's bed, hugging them both close to her. "There's no bad man here," she said. "You're both safe now. Nothing's going to happen to you."

And not just because of Cash protecting them, but because she would do her best as well to keep them safe. From danger and from the heartbreak their own father might cause them.

The heartbreak Valentina had suffered when

they'd separated, and then without trying to patch things up, he'd had her served with divorce papers.

She wouldn't let him hurt and disappoint their daughters the way that he had her. While Cash protected them from danger, she would have to figure out how to protect Luci and Ana from the potential heartbreak of getting too attached to him.

Like Valentina had…

So much so that that text hadn't been wrong. She was sad whenever she thought of him, which over the past three years had been all too often. Maybe that was because she saw him every time she looked at their daughters. She saw him in Luci's vivid green eyes and in the curve of Ana's lips when she smiled and with the intensity they both showed when they listened to a story Valentina read or when she told them about something that had happened at the library.

They were such good little girls. So sweet.

They had to be safe.

Ana clutched at her, her chubby fingers grasping the torn sleeve of Valentina's dress and the scraped skin beneath it. Valentina bit her lip to hold back a cry of pain.

"Bad man," the little girl murmured again.

Was she talking about the one who'd been driving the car? Or Cash? Had he scared her too badly when he'd picked up the stroller?

"The man who picked up you two and carried you back here in the stroller, he is a good man," she assured them.

He's your father...

But she couldn't tell them that until she'd talked to Cash, until he'd told her what he planned to do about them. Did he just intend to protect them from this serial killer? Or did he want to be part of their lives?

"Fib," Luci said. "He a fib…"

A lie? Valentina was the one who'd lied, at least by omission. She hadn't told Cash about them, and she hadn't told them about Cash. While they'd been curious when they'd seen other kids with their dads at the day care or on the playground, they'd never asked about theirs. Maybe because he'd never been around…

"Where the fib?" Luci asked.

Then Valentina remembered when she'd told them when they'd been so shy with him when they'd first gotten back to the condo. "FBI agent," she said. "Yes, he's a good man."

"Like a poly man," Ana added.

Realizing the toddler was trying to say policeman, Valentina smiled and nodded. While the twins were very smart for their ages, they also had slight speech impediments that made them a little harder to understand. "Yes."

"Where is he?" Luci asked, and she glanced around the room now like Valentina had.

"He left for a little while," she said, "but he will be coming back soon." She wasn't sure if that was a good thing or a bad thing. But then she heard the sound of male voices, loud male voices, coming from her front door, and she wished he was here now. In-

side with them, to protect them like he'd promised her
he would because neither of those voices she could
hear was Cash's.

Was someone trying to get past the police officer, trying to get inside, to get to her and the girls?

Cash had made her turn the dead bolt behind him
when he'd left. But that didn't mean the lock would
keep out whoever was out there arguing with the officer. Locks and doors could be broken.

Just like hearts…

Valentina wasn't going to take a chance, not
with her daughters. "Let's play hide-and-seek," she
told them, infusing fake excitement into her voice;
maybe it would disguise the fear she was really feeling. "Let's hide so well that nobody can find us…"

The condo wasn't that big, though; they wouldn't
be able to hide for long before they were found.

Chapter 6

Cash's shadow in the dark had never materialized. While he'd heard the person, he hadn't seen him. So he'd taken his time driving back to Valentina's place, making sure he wasn't followed. Not that the person who'd tried running them down didn't know where Valentina lived, or he probably wouldn't have known what street they'd be crossing and when...

He had to have been tracking her. How else would the text writer have known how sad she was?

Unless that had been a bluff. Unless the texter and the driver of the car weren't the same? While Cash couldn't imagine who else it could be, he hadn't wanted to take any chances, so he'd made certain nobody followed him.

And so he'd been gone longer than he'd wanted to

be, longer than he should have been, because when the elevator doors opened onto her floor, he could hear the yelling. Two men, voices raised, argued hotly.

"You need to turn around and leave," Dave advised, his voice shaking with fury.

"I need to see Valentina!" the other man shouted. "I need to know what's going on!"

"It's late," Dave replied. "You need to leave."

"I need to know what the hell you're doing here!" the guy hurled back at him.

"Why?" Cash asked the question as he reached beneath his jacket, his fingers close to the gun handle sticking out of the holster. He'd already drawn his weapon too many times today. The first had been as a desperate measure to save Valentina and the girls.

The second had been out of paranoia, probably, since he hadn't actually seen anyone else in the parking garage earlier. Maybe some dumb kid had been about to try to mug him and had quickly changed his mind and career choice when he'd seen the gun. Either way, Cash didn't want to overreact now, especially if this guy had a reason for so desperately wanting to see Valentina. Was he dating Cash's ex-wife?

Cash studied the guy, whose face was flushed as if he'd been drinking or maybe just because he was angry. He wasn't quite as tall as Cash and probably a little older with dark eyes and a mouth drawn into a tight grimace of annoyance.

"Why what?" he asked Cash.

"Why are you so desperate to see Valentina at…"

He glanced at his watch. He'd thought it was later than nine; it felt later to him and it had already been dark when he'd driven back over here, dark in the parking garage, too, as if some of the lights had burned out. But nine o'clock on a Friday night wasn't really late, especially not if this man had had plans with Valentina.

A date?

She hadn't mentioned anything earlier, but they'd had so much else to talk about that it could have easily slipped her mind. Cash felt a small jolt of satisfaction if she'd forgotten her date. And a small stab of jealousy that she might have had one.

But that was crazy. Of course she'd dated over the past three years. She was too beautiful and smart and funny not to have men chasing after her.

Men like this guy?

"Who are you?" Cash asked him. But he wanted more than his name; he wanted to know the man's relationship to Cash's wife. Ex-wife…

The guy looked from Dave to him and back. "The question is what's going on? Why are you two lurking outside Valentina's door?"

Valentina. So they were on a first-name basis.

"How do you know her?" Cash asked, and he wasn't sure he was asking as an investigator or as the man who'd once loved Valentina, who'd been married to her. But they'd been divorced as long as they'd been married, so he really had no right, except that she was in danger and he wanted to protect her. At least that was the excuse he gave himself and he would give her if she asked why he was interrogating her date.

The guy narrowed his eyes. "What's going on?"

"Why won't you answer any questions?" Cash asked. He nodded at Dave, who pulled out his shield and showed the guy.

"The police!" the guy exclaimed. "Oh, my God, why didn't you tell me who you are and what you're doing here?" He asked Dave that question before he turned back to Cash. "And if he's the police, who the hell are you?"

Dave, who'd clearly lost his patience with the guy, snorted. "You have the potential to get in a lot more trouble with him than you have with me if you don't do what I told you to and back off right now."

But the man was bristling with belligerence and stepped closer to them both, closer to the door, as if he was going to shove his way inside. "What's going on?" he persisted, almost desperately. "Is Valentina all right? And the girls? Those little girls of hers?" His face was more flushed now, his eyes looking a bit glassy with unshed tears or maybe inebriation.

Cash didn't know what to think of the guy. "Who are you?" he repeated his question. "And you better damn well answer me or Sergeant Percell here will be booking you—"

"Blake Highland," the guy finally replied, blurting out his name.

"And how do you know Valentina?" Cash asked, and he held his breath now as he waited for the answer, as he had earlier when he'd asked Valentina if he was the father of her twins.

The guy pointed toward a door down the hall. "I live on the same floor. I keep an eye out for her, single mom living alone with those little girls."

They were vulnerable and an easy target for a serial killer and for men like this neighbor of hers. Pushy guys who got pushier when they'd been drinking like this guy must have been. Cash was close enough that he could smell the scent of liquor wafting from his mouth.

Highland shook his head. "Poor Valentina. The dad of those girls is a deadbeat..."

Deadbeat. The word was like a blow to Cash's gut, making him feel physically ill. Deadbeat. This guy probably wasn't the only one who thought so, who wondered why she had no help with the kids, financial or otherwise.

"He's never around. She handles everything on her own," Blake Highland continued. "It's a damn shame. She deserves better. She's a really sweet, hardworking lady and a great mother." His lips curved into a faint smile. "And she's pretty damn hot, too."

Pride stinging from that deadbeat comment, Cash asked, "So is that why you're hanging around outside her door? Why you're harassing her?"

The guy sucked in a breath now like he'd been punched. "No. I saw this guy hanging around her—"

"This guy is a police officer," Cash reminded him.

"So what's happened? What's going on?" Highland demanded to know. "Are they okay?"

Cash glanced toward the door. Were they?

Since he'd heard the arguing the minute the elevator doors had opened, Valentina must have heard them, too, since they were right outside her door.

He reached around Dave and knocked. "Valentina?"

He didn't want to wake the girls, but he couldn't imagine they'd slept through the arguing, either. And he doubted Valentina had gone to bed yet. So why wasn't she unlocking the dead bolt he'd made her turn as he'd been leaving earlier?

There was only one way in and one way out, right? He hadn't checked out the place as thoroughly as he should have before he'd left, but that was what he'd remembered from when Valentina had shown him the condo when she'd first inherited it. She'd been so excited about it, had wanted to live there so badly, but he'd shut her down with the excuse that it was too far from his office and her job at the time. Just as he'd shut her down about starting a family.

She had it anyway.

He knocked harder. "Valentina. It's safe for you to open the door now."

Maybe it was him she didn't want to let back in; she hadn't been thrilled that he'd wanted to stay at the condo to protect them. But she hadn't been able to argue that it wasn't necessary, either, not after that car had nearly run down her and the girls.

He hadn't been there for them the first few years of their lives, but now that he knew about them, and knew that they needed him, he intended to be there now.

If Valentina would let him in…

She didn't want to let him in again. Not into the condo and definitely not into her life and the lives of her daughters. Their daughters. While they were hiding yet, she could hear them giggling together because, of course, they had stuck together. They never hid separately from each other even when playing hide-and-seek with just her. Even though they didn't know it, they were playing hide-and-seek now with someone else, with whoever she had heard arguing out the door.

Probably Cash's friend and…

She hadn't recognized the other voice. But she identified Cash's the minute he'd joined them. She recognized it now as he called her name and told her it was safe for her to let him in. But it wasn't safe. Even though he claimed he wanted to protect them, she knew that he would eventually wind up hurting them himself. When he left…

Because he would. He wouldn't stay with them here on Coney Island and play happy family; he'd made that clear to her three years ago. So that was why she didn't open the door when he called out to her. She stood in front of it, her fingers on the dead bolt.

"Valentina, are you all right?" he asked, his voice lower as if he knew she was standing there, as if he felt her presence like she felt his.

She'd always been so damn aware of him, so at-tuned to him and attracted. And because she knew him and his overdeveloped sense of responsibility and protectiveness, she knew he would break down the door if she didn't open it. So she turned the dead bolt and let him in. Again.

He didn't step fully inside, though, just stood on the threshold as if trying to keep her in the condo and the other two men out in the hall. One must have been his friend and the other was one of Valentina's neighbors.

Blake…something; she couldn't remember his last name. She usually tried to avoid him because he made her uncomfortable with the way he looked at her, as he was looking at her now, with that glazed-eye gleam in his eyes. She'd learned over the past three years that some men preyed on single mothers, thinking they would be grateful for whatever atten-tion a man chose to give them. Valentina preferred for men like that to show her no attention at all.

She especially hated how Blake timed his drop-in visits for after the girls were in bed and after he'd been drinking. "I asked you to stop coming over," she reminded him now.

The guy's face flushed. "I saw this person loiter-ing in the hall outside your door, and I was worried about you," he said as if he deserved a medal.

He was one of those guys who wanted everyone else to think he was a good guy, a hero, when he was really just a shallow opportunist.

He was the opposite of Cash, who'd always been

reluctant to tell others what he did for a living. He was a true hero who didn't want anyone to know that he was.

Maybe for reasons like this...

So his *sad ex-wife* didn't get threatened.

"I'm fine," she insisted.

"But something must have happened for the police to be here. Are the girls okay?"

As if he really cared. He never paid them any attention when they saw him in the hall or elevator.

"They're fine," she insisted. But she wondered how long they would stay hiding before they came out to see who was at the door. "You have no reason to worry about me."

The guy looked from the police officer to Cash again. Then he remarked, "You never told me who you were. Another cop?"

The other man, who must have been Cash's police friend Dave even though he wasn't in a uniform, snorted. "He's FBI, man."

Valentina swallowed a groan, fearing her neighbor's reaction to that news.

His eyes widened. "FBI? What the hell's going on, Valentina? You gotta let the co-op know if you're putting all of us in danger."

She did not need to get in trouble with the co-op board. Several of her neighbors had already been upset that a young single mother with active toddlers had replaced the prior owners, the quiet, sweet old couple that were her grandparents. They'd died during the pandemic, as they'd done everything, together, holding hands between their hospital beds.

She'd wanted a relationship like that for herself. Like her grandparents and like her parents who were traveling in their retirement, determined to enjoy every minute of life they had left together.

"Nobody is in danger," she assured Blake. At least not physical danger at the moment.

Blake shook his head, refusing to accept her claim. "The police and the FBI don't get involved unless it's big—"

"I'm her husband," Cash said. Before Valentina could correct him to add the ex, he continued, "You know. The deadbeat dad."

That was what Blake must have called him. But it wasn't Cash's fault that he hadn't been around; it was hers. Would he have come around even if he'd known about them?

Just before she'd left, he'd made it absolutely clear to her that he never wanted to become a father; he never wanted to have a family. She suspected he hadn't wanted a wife, either.

She wasn't sure even now why he'd married her. But they'd had so much passion, and she believed they'd been so in love. At least she had been. And because of that passion and love, she hadn't asked him the questions she should have before they got married. And even when he'd first told her he didn't want kids, she'd figured he would eventually change his mind. That he would want to share their love with children.

"Come out! Come out wherever you are!" a little voice called from the direction of their bedrooms.

A smile tugged at Valentina's lips. She was the one who was supposed to say that when they were hiding. Not the other way around, but sometimes they forgot the rules. Today, of all days, with the car nearly running them down, with Cash saving them, with taking a nap before dinner, they were going to be distracted and confused.

Like she was...

So she didn't protest when Cash slid his arm around her waist and drew her close to his side. "You and your neighbors have nothing to worry about," he told Blake Highland. "There is no threat to anyone in the building." But the way he narrowed his eyes and the hard stare he sent the other man suggested otherwise, especially when he added, "Just remember and respect what Valentina told you, you need to *stop* dropping by."

Blake raised his chin and returned Cash's stare with a hard, resentful one of his own. "Yeah, well, I was only looking out for her like a lot of the other neighbors do."

Valentina acknowledged that some of them did. The ones who'd known and loved her grandparents like she had. They didn't judge or resent her or want to take advantage of her. They even offered to babysit sometimes for the girls when she had to run out quickly for something.

This man she wouldn't have trusted alone with her girls and especially not alone with herself. So she was glad she hadn't pointed out that Cash was her ex, especially when the guy finally turned around and walked away, slightly unsteady on his feet.

Cash turned then to his friend who gave him a sharp nod. "I'll check him out."

"Thanks," Cash said. "And thanks for standing guard until I got back."

"I can stay," Dave offered.

"I appreciate the offer," Cash said, but he shook his head. "But go home. You weren't even on duty today. Enjoy the rest of your evening."

"Thank you," Valentina added, and forced a smile when really she wanted to call him back, wanted him to stay and for Cash to leave.

But Cash had dropped a duffel bag on the floor when he'd stepped inside, and his arm was still looped around her waist, familiarly, possessively. Clearly he was determined to stay even if his friend did.

Of course she could have refused to let Cash back in the condo at all. She could have insisted that they were perfectly safe inside with the door deadbolted. But she didn't feel safe, not after what had happened today, what could have happened to her and the girls. She didn't feel safe with Cash here, either, though.

A soft voice called again, "Come out! Come out wherever you are…"

And she knew it wasn't fair to them or to Cash to keep them apart any longer than she already had. She felt guilty about that, because she'd done so mostly to protect herself. To protect her heart.

But she had believed she'd been protecting the girls, too, from Cash rejecting them or disappointing them. But if Cash hadn't shown up when he had today, she might have lost them forever. She might have lost her own life as well. So instead of pulling away and pushing him out the door with his friend, she leaned against him, grateful for the support of his arm around her, of his strong body against hers.

And she wondered which was the bigger mistake that she'd made.

Never telling him about the girls.

Or letting him stay…

Chapter 7

Cash could have lost his daughters today without ever knowing they existed. He could have lost them without ever seeing their sweet faces and hearing their soft, giggly little voices.

That knowledge wrapped around Cash's heart, squeezing it so tightly that he sucked in a breath over the sharp pain. He *looked* for them now, opening closet doors, peering behind curtains.

But from the giggling, he knew where they were. Under Valentina's bed…

"Come out, come out wherever you are." He said it now like they had called out just moments ago.

Valentina had tried to pull away from him to find them, but he'd held on to her a moment longer because her body had felt so damn good against him.

Her warmth, her softness and the sweet scent of her honeysuckle perfume had overwhelmed him, and he hadn't wanted to let her go.

Again…

But he was the one who released her, just as he had three years ago. "Wait," he'd said, before she could rush off toward the sounds of giggling. "Let me find them."

"You might scare them," she'd warned him. "They're really very shy."

"You told them that I'm a good guy," he'd replied. "Remember?"

And her face flushed as if she was embarrassed or maybe frustrated. Did she consider him a good guy? Or did she hate him for refusing to compromise in their marriage and for divorcing her when she'd left?

She must hate him, or she would have told him about her pregnancy. She would have let him be a father to the child, children, she was carrying. Unless she'd really believed that he would reject them, that he wouldn't want to be a part of their lives.

He had missed so much of that already. And he should hate her for that, but he couldn't. He understood her reasons, which were the very reasons he had given her for ending their marriage.

Because he hadn't wanted to be a father…

When she'd first brought up starting a family, he'd used the explanation he'd heard other childless people use: *I don't want to bring a child into such a dangerous and evil world.*

As an FBI special agent in the serial killer unit,

he knew better than most just how evil and dangerous the world was. And after today, after she and the girls had nearly been killed, Valentina had to realize that he was right.

But the girls were here now. So all he could do was his very best to keep them safe. Tears had stung his eyes, and he'd implored her, "Let me find them."

Her dark eyes had glistened as she'd nodded. "Okay."

And so he'd followed the sounds of giggling through the living room to the short hall. He passed the open door to their very pink bedroom and pushed open the one that had been left ajar to Valentina's room.

It smelled like her, like honeysuckle and sunshine, but the walls and bedding and furniture were all white. The color was in the pillows and the decorations, which were all bright pops of orange and deep green like the shag rug on the dark wood floor. He dropped down onto it and peered under the bed.

Two sets of eyes stared back at him. The dark ones that were so like Valentina's and the green eyes that were so like his. He opened his mouth to talk to them but realized that he didn't even know their names.

And they didn't know his. They didn't know that he was their daddy.

"You da fib," one little girl murmured as she worm-crawled toward him.

"Da fib?"

"FBI," Valentina said from where she stood in the

doorway, as if she hadn't trusted him alone with their daughters. "Remember, we told them who you are."

"I want to tell them what else I am," he said, his heart pounding so hard and fast that it was as if it was going to burst if he didn't then reveal that he was also their father.

"You and I need to talk about that first," she said.

Did she not want them to know?

Why?

But then he realized she was worried that he wasn't going to stick around, that he would disappoint and let them down like he had her during their marriage. And that worry settled heavily in the pit of his stomach; he didn't want to hurt them, either.

"Do you wanna hide now?" the little girl asked as she rolled out from beneath the bed.

It was the one with the green eyes that matched his. Her twin crawled closer but stayed under the bed yet and a little behind her sister, as if she was shy or scared.

He didn't want them to be scared of him or of that bad man, but he didn't want to lie to them, either. "Not yet," he said. "But I will take a turn another time." He was going to be there a while, which would give him time to get to know his daughters. But he wanted even more to catch the Landmark Killer than he already had.

He had more of a reason to catch him now that the psychopath had threatened Cash's family. But had it really been the Landmark Killer who had come after them?

Why would he have gone after two little girls and their mother? Unless their names somehow would help him spell out his idol's.

"What are your names?" he asked them.

"Luci," the green-eyed one replied.

"Luciana," Valentina added. "And Ana."

There were an *L* and two *A*s in Maeve O'Leary's name, but the girls definitely didn't fit the description of the other victims: blond, blue-eyed men in their thirties. Maybe nearly running them down had just been a warning to Cash, intending to make him back off from the investigation, which was probably what he'd intended with that text: to distract him. But trying to run down the girls and Valentina had taken it much further. Unless the driver behind the wheel of that stolen car hadn't been the serial killer and maybe had had nothing to do with the Landmark Killer at all.

Whatever the driver's motivation was, the girls were definitely in danger.

"Luciana and Ana," he repeated, and turned back toward Valentina. "Your grandmother and mom's names."

"Ana's middle name is Michaela for your dad," she said.

A pang of loss struck his heart. Over her honoring his dad, Michael, in that way, and because he'd had no part in naming them. He cleared his throat and asked, "And their last name?"

While she'd honored his father, had she made it

clear that Cash was their father? Or had she intended to keep him entirely out of their children's lives?

"Acosta—"

He sucked in a breath.

"Acosta Colton," she finished.

"Casa Colton," Ana murmured, and her eyelids were beginning to droop, her little chin dropping back onto the carpet. She'd scooted half out from under the bed but was still partially beneath it. Maybe she felt safer there after what had happened today.

The car. The loud voices in the hallway.

Luci was sitting on the floor next to him, and she reached out and touched his hand. "Did you get 'im?"

"Get who?" Cash asked, and he reached out to tickle her tummy. "You? I got you…"

She giggled and wriggled away from him. "Not me. I not bad. Did you get the bad man?"

Cash tensed. "Bad man?" Had the little girls witnessed more than he'd realized? "Did you see him? What did he look like?" Maybe they had seen more than he had. "Was he wearing a mask?" Maybe the driver hadn't been wearing it that first time he'd tried to run them down; maybe he'd only put it on when he'd turned around and tried for them again. "What do you remember about him? About the bad man?"

His voice must have gotten too sharp, because the little girl's bottom lip started to quiver, and tears filled her green eyes.

"I'm sorry," he said. "I didn't mean to make you cry."

She didn't start crying, but Ana did, tears rolling down her face from her closed eyes.

And he remembered it wasn't just because he was a workaholic that he hadn't wanted to have kids or because he hadn't wanted to bring any innocent children into an evil world. It was because he wasn't good with them.

Every interaction with his friends' kids or with young witnesses, he'd bungled. He tended to scare them with his intensity, as he just had his own daughters. When his cell rang, he jumped up for the floor and rushed out of the room. Not to take the call but to give him a moment alone, because making those girls cry had tears stinging his own eyes.

And now he totally understood Valentina's hesitation over telling them that he was their father. She definitely had reason to worry about him hurting them.

Alarm gripped Valentina. She was used to her daughters' tears, especially when they were as tired and hungry as they probably were now. She'd figured out when they were babies the reasons that they cried. They weren't crying now because they were tired or hungry. They were crying because they were afraid, and feeling that fear in them worried her. But she hadn't felt it just in them but in Cash as well when he'd fled from the room.

Sure, he'd had a call coming in on his cell, but she didn't hear him talking to anyone outside the room.

Had he just used the call as an excuse to get away from the girls?

Or was it just that his work would always come first like it had in their marriage? That call was probably from someone in his FBI special unit. Or maybe from his friend from the local precinct.

She should actually be relieved that he was working this case so hard, that he would catch the bad man like Luci had asked him.

She took his place on the carpet next to the bed and pulled both girls into her arms. "Shh…" she murmured. "You don't have to worry about the bad man."

She was worried enough for all of them, and clearly Cash was worried, too. But firing questions at them the way he had about what they'd seen had only scared them more than they had already been.

"It's okay," she assured them, holding their trembling bodies against hers. If only she could hold them forever, keep them safe in her arms.

But the world didn't work like that. Cash had pointed that out to her when she'd told him that she wanted to start a family with him. He'd shown her all the horrible statistics about crime and dangers of the world, and then he'd asked how she could bring children into it.

But how could she not? Didn't the world need more good in it to combat that evil, to fight it like he was fighting it?

And her children were so good, so sweet. And while it wasn't their reason for crying, they were tired and hungry right now, too. She could hear one of their bellies rumbling, and an echo of it coming from the other one.

"Okay, you two, go wash up, and I will make us something to eat."

"'roni and cheese," Ana requested.

"Pancakes," Luci said.

"Pancakes for beckfast?" Ana queried with a giggle snort.

"Dinner, too," Luci said.

Sometimes they did have breakfast for dinner, but Valentina was already worried about Cash judging her parenting so she wanted to fix something healthier, especially as they were going to bed soon.

Fortunately she had some leftover turkey tetrazzini that would heat up fast and that the girls actually loved. While they headed into her bathroom to clean up, she stepped into the hall where Cash was leaning against the wall.

She pressed a hand to her heart, which pounded fast with surprise. "I didn't know you were standing there. I thought you had a call…" She'd suspected then he'd used it as an excuse to escape from his crying daughters.

His face flushed a bit. "It was Ashlynn. I need to call her back."

But clearly he'd been waiting to do that.

"Are you going to tell her…about them?" she wondered. She'd loved Cash's family and would have loved to maintain relationships with them after the divorce, but it had been easier for her to cut ties with all the Coltons completely. She'd figured it was the only way she would get over Cash.

She wasn't sure that it had worked, though, because her heart hadn't slowed from its frantic beating. Maybe that wasn't because of him but because of the situation. The entire dangerous out-of-control situation.

"Before I tell any of my family about them, I want to tell the girls first," he said. "I want them to know that I'm their father."

Valentina's heart rate quickened even more, and panic overwhelmed her, making it hard to breathe. "I—I…" She couldn't deal with this right now. "Not tonight," she implored him. "It's getting late. They haven't eaten yet, and they need to go back to bed and sleep."

And hopefully not wake up with another nightmare like the one Ana had had earlier during her brief nap.

He levered himself away from the wall then and stepped closer to her, so close that she could feel the heat and strength of his body. A body she'd once loved so much…

She'd loved his strong arms wrapped around her, holding her close. His chest where she would lay her head to sleep at night, on the nights he hadn't spent in the office, working on some case, on finding some killer.

That was all he was doing here: working. Protecting them from one of the serial killers he'd devoted his life to hunt.

"This feels like you're stalling, Valentina," he said. "Don't you think three years was long enough to do that? Or did you never intend to tell me at all?"

She really wasn't sure. Maybe when the girls asked, she would have told them then. And if she'd told them, she would have had to let him know as well in case they'd wanted to meet him.

Or maybe not…

She shrugged.

"Do you hate me that much?" Cash asked. "That you would purposely keep them from me?"

No. That was the problem. She'd loved him too much. Too much to ever get over him if she'd had to see him regularly over the years.

But even as much as she'd loved him, she loved her daughters more.

"I was just trying to do the same thing you're trying now," she said.

His brow furrowed. "What?"

"To protect them."

He flinched. "I would never—"

"Not purposely," she agreed. "But you would…" Just like he had hurt her.

"Valentina…" He stepped even closer then until their bodies touched, and his tensed.

Hers softened with desire. A desire she hadn't felt in so many years. Since Cash.

She stared up at him as he stared down her, and the way he looked at her was how he used to, with so much desire, with so much…

No. She couldn't think it was love, not now, or he

wouldn't have divorced her as quickly as he had. He would have tried to work things out.

Maybe it was just lust, and maybe that was all she was feeling, too. That had her pulse racing, was making it hard to breathe and had heat rushing through her.

He was so damn handsome, and she wanted to reach out, wanted to skim her fingertips over the softness of his beard. She wanted to feel that against her face, his lips pressed to hers…

He might have wanted it, too. His chest was moving as if he was having trouble breathing. He started to lean down, lowering his head toward hers.

But then little giggles rang out from the bathroom with the sound of splashing. And his cell phone vibrated again.

"You better take that," she said. "And I better save my bathroom…" She stepped around him to head back into her bedroom. But she stopped just inside the door, her legs, and she needed a moment to collect herself and to remind her that he was only here because of a killer.

Ashlynn's hand was shaking as she held her ringing cell. If it went to voice mail this time, she was going to go to Valentina's condo. That had to be where Cash was since his cell phone was pinging off a tower on Coney Island. She was close, had ridden with their brother Patrick out to this scene, this abandoned parking lot.

She was scared, but not for herself. She was scared for Cash and Valentina and the girls.

Were they okay?

Had something happened?

"Hey."

Cash's voice suddenly emanating from the speaker startled her, and Ashlynn nearly dropped her phone. "Thank God," she murmured. "I thought something had happened…"

"Not here," he said, then cleared his throat as if it was a lie he was having trouble swallowing.

"Fib…" A child's voice emanated from Ashlynn's cell now, as if a kid was calling out Cash on his lie.

One of her daughters. Had they already bonded with Cash enough to call him a liar? "You're at Valentina's?" she asked, just to confirm.

"Yeah, I'm going to be staying here for a bit to make sure nothing happens to her or the twins."

The twins? Not *his* twins. Did he know? She did; after talking to him earlier, she'd pulled their birth certificates. Maybe he did know; maybe that was why he was staying there to protect them.

"That's good," she said. Because they needed protection. She drew in a sharp breath, then coughed and sputtered as the smoke burned her throat.

"Where are you?" he asked her. "And why are you calling?"

She glanced around the parking lot of the abandoned warehouse. It didn't look all that abandoned now with firefighters and police officers and crime scene techs hovering around the smoldering metal of a burned car.

"I think we found the car that was used to nearly run you down," she said.

Cash's ragged sigh of relief rattled the cell speaker. "That's great. Thank God. What did you learn? Any prints? DNA?"

She sighed now. "No. And whoever it was made sure that there wouldn't be anything left behind to trace back to him. He torched it."

"Sometimes there is still a print or something..."

"Sometimes," she agreed. "But according to Patrick, this was a hot fire with a lot of accelerants." As cohead of the FBI's CSI, he was the expert. He could have trusted someone else to come out, but he'd wanted to check this out himself because it involved Cash. He was suited up, checking out the burned shell of that car. "I don't think we'll find anything. Whoever this is, they know what they're doing, Cash. They're professional."

"A hit man?" he asked. "Is that what you're saying?"

"Just someone who's done this before," she said. Like a serial killer determined not to get caught or someone in law enforcement who knew the ins and outs of investigations. "Or has been on the other side of this."

"One of us," Cash murmured.

"Law enforcement maybe," Ashlynn admitted, although she didn't want to believe someone within the FBI or a local precinct could be responsible for murders. "You need to be careful," she told him.

"You, too."

She hadn't gotten one of those texts that her twin brothers and her cousin Sinead had received. But none of them had fit the description of the killer's victims. He was fixated on blond men. Those were the victims whose lives he'd taken.

So why go after Valentina?

Just to mess with Cash? Or was there someone else after her for another reason?

"Have you talked to Valentina over the past three years?" she asked. If he'd known those kids were his, he would have. Wouldn't he? "Do you know what she's been doing?"

While Brennan had received a weird text like Cash had, it hadn't been the Landmark Killer who'd gone after the woman Brennan had been falling for but someone else who'd wanted to kill her and very nearly had.

"Could there be someone else after Valentina?" she asked. "Someone who might want to hurt her?"

"Valentina?" he asked, as if the thought of anyone wanting to hurt her was inexplicable.

It was to Ashlynn, too. "You know the world we live in," she reminded him. "Dangerous people go after innocent people all the time. They actually seem to prey on them."

He made a strange, strangled sounding noise… either a grunt of agreement or a gasp.

"Gobble, gobble," a little voice murmured out of the speaker. "Turkey for beckfast."

Cash chuckled then.

That was a sound Ashlynn hadn't heard him make in way too long. She smiled. The kids sounded adorable, and knowing how beautiful Valentina was, they were probably cute. And they were Coltons, too. For some reason Coltons seemed to attract danger.

Her heart rate quickened. "Cash—"

"I have to go now," he cut her off. "Let me know if you find anything more out about the car."

Then he disconnected the call, leaving Ashlynn as scared as she'd been when he first hadn't picked up. Even now that she knew where he was, she wasn't convinced that he was safe…that he, Valentina or her nieces would ever be safe until this killer was caught.

Chapter 8

Cash dreamed of danger, and not from careening vehicles or gunshots but from giggling little girls. And their mother.

Beautiful, patient, so very good with them during dinner and throughout their baths and then tucking them into bed with those stories again.

He dreamed of every moment, savoring it, as he considered all the moments he'd missed. And that hurt so damn bad.

That was the danger. Wanting this forever...

Wanting them forever.

But if Valentina still wanted him, she wouldn't have signed those divorce papers and kept his children from him. While she'd let him spend the night, on the couch, he knew it was just because she wanted to keep the girls safe as badly as he did.

She wouldn't take any chances with their well-being, which was why she didn't want to tell them who he was. Their father...

She didn't trust him.

He could understand that; he trusted few people himself. Even now he wasn't sleeping deeply. He stayed aware enough to notice the shift in the air around him, the faint vibration of footfalls on the floor beneath the couch on which he lay. And he felt the intense gaze of someone watching him.

He reached beneath the blanket that Valentina had given him, touching the handle of the gun in the holster he wore. He hadn't taken off his clothes or his weapon, worried that he might need to act quickly if something happened. If that person came for them again...

A pro.

Ashlynn had warned him that was what she and Patrick thought the person was: a professional criminal. Killer. Or someone with inside knowledge of investigations. His unit had already determined that about the Landmark Killer, that he had to be close to them.

Too close...

Like whoever was watching Cash sleep.

Then he heard a little giggle, and a smile tugged at his lips as he opened his eyes. The twins were standing at the end of the couch, peering over the arm at him. And behind them stood Valentina, her beautiful hair mussed, her face flushed from sleep and maybe because she'd been staring, too. Like she'd stared at him last night when they'd been alone in the hall and he'd been so tempted to kiss her…and he might have if the girls hadn't started giggling.

"Mornin', seepy head," Luci greeted him.

And he chuckled. They were so cute.

"You seeped over," Ana added.

He wanted to scoop them up and hold them close like Valentina had last night as she'd comforted them. He didn't know how to do that, how to interact with them naturally. While he wanted to blame Valentina for that, for denying him a presence in their lives, he knew that was on him. He'd never been good with kids.

"You probably didn't get much sleep on the couch," Valentina remarked.

He shoved his fingers through his hair, which felt like it was standing on end. "It wasn't the couch." He'd not slept well for so many other reasons, the biggest one being so close to her again.

Seeing her…

Smelling her…

Wanting her as passionately as he always had.

But she was in danger even as his ex. If they were together…

She would be in more danger, and so would Cash. He would be in danger of disappointing the girls just as he had her so many times. Late for dinner. Canceling anniversary trips.

Not making her feel as special as she deserved to

feel. She was so beautiful, even with the dark circles beneath her eyes that hinted at her not getting any more sleep than he had.

She touched her face, as if self-conscious of his staring. Then she turned away and headed toward the kitchen. The girls stayed behind, still studying him over the arm of the couch. And his heart yearned to tell them the truth.

He wanted them to know who he was, what his relationship to them was. "We never had that conversation I wanted to have," he said to Valentina as he got up from the couch and folded the blanket he'd used.

He heard her suck in a breath and she peered at him over the kitchen island, her dark eyes imploring him. "Let me get some coffee first."

The kitchen was in a corner of the open space that encompassed the living room and dining room, too. The cabinets were white and so were the counters, but like her bedroom, there were pops of color in the reclaimed glass backsplash and in the teal pots and pans that dangled from a copper pot rack over that counter. There was also a teal coffeepot, which was currently brewing, and other small teal appliances.

He smiled. "You're still not a morning person?"

She glared at him. "No. But these two are, like you always were."

Were they like him? If so, it had to be from genetics, since he hadn't been part of their lives. He hadn't been able to nurture them.

But it was clear that Valentina had.

They joined her in the kitchen. "Helping" her with

"beckfast," which was pulling boxes of cereal from a cupboard and a bag of bread from the counter. A small step stool was pushed against the cupboard, and they both tried to climb onto it to put bread in the toaster.

Valentina moved around them, moderated their argument and made the breakfast as if performing a waltz. With grace and patience and affection...

She was a great mother. The mother he'd always suspected she would be. That was why he'd filed those divorce papers, so that she could have this family she'd always wanted. The family he hadn't wanted to give her.

But yet he had. And he wasn't sure what to do about it, what to do about this feeling of being on the outside looking in...like he was Scrooge and a ghost was showing him what his future could have been had he made better choices.

At the time, he'd thought he'd done the right thing. But now, he had no idea what to think and worried that if he didn't protect them from the danger they were facing, he was going to see the consequences of bad decisions and of bad things happening to Valentina and the girls.

Because of him.

While Valentina had made breakfast, Cash insisted on cleaning up with the girls. She could hear the deep rumble of his voice and their giggles as well as the rushing water of the faucet.

Her heart had yearned for this for so long, to have

this family with him, share these moments with him and their children. But when she'd told him she wanted to have children, he'd used his job, hunting serial killers, as an excuse not to have a family, not to give her what she'd wanted. So it was kind of ironic that he was only here now because of the serial killer's implied threat, not because Cash wanted to be here.

Not because he wanted to be with her and their daughters.

She wasn't sure what he wanted. The way he looked at her, with all that heat in his green eyes, reminded her of the past, of the passion that had burned so hot between them. So hot that it had probably been inevitable they would get burned alive from it.

Her knees trembled a bit, and she leaned back against the wall of her bedroom, next to the open door through which she eavesdropped. She didn't entirely trust him not to tell the girls that he was their father.

And she couldn't really blame him if he did. She had denied him his rights for too long already. To continue to put off the moment of truth was probably unfair to him and to their children. She just didn't know how to tell them, how to explain what she couldn't even really explain herself.

But maybe it was better to do it now, before the girls were old enough to understand what she'd done and hated her for it. Like Cash probably hated her…

She heard more giggling, louder, closer, and footsteps running. She forced a smile, expecting the girls to burst into her room as they always did, but the running stopped at their bedroom and the door slammed shut. She stepped away from her wall to go out and see what had had them running like that, but a big, hard body blocked her doorway.

"Oh…" She nearly slammed into Cash's chest. The T-shirt he wore beneath an open-collared shirt was molded to every muscle of it right now, the cotton soaked. His hair was wet, too. "I thought you were washing the dishes." She tried to fight the smile tugging at her mouth.

"Apparently I looked like a dirty mug," he remarked with a grin. He touched his beard, which looked as damp as his hair and shirt.

She found herself giving in to the temptation she'd fought last night, and she reached out, running her fingers over the damp, soft hair of his beard and over the rigid jaw beneath it. "Your mug looks pretty clean now," she murmured. And just pretty…

She'd always thought he was one of the most attractive men she'd ever seen, since that first day he had walked into the library where she'd worked in Manhattan. He'd been looking for something, some obscure book written by a suspected serial killer.

She'd found it for him. Even after he'd caught and put away that serial killer, he'd kept coming back to see her, and they'd started dating. They'd only been going out for a little while before he'd proposed, and they'd had their whirlwind wedding on Coney Island.

She blinked against the sudden sting of tears in her eyes as she remembered the beauty and promise of that day. How naive she'd been to think they would live happily ever after...

"What's wrong?" he asked, and his hand covered hers on his face, holding it there against his beard.

"What's right?" she asked. "I feel like that car hit me yesterday." And had knocked the sense completely out of her so that she wanted to kiss her ex-husband, wanted to be with him like they'd once been.

Happy.

Passionate.

In love...

No. *She'd* been in love. If he'd loved her as much as she had him, he would have tried to make it work, tried to find a way that they could stay together. That was why she'd left, so she could take some time to clear her head and try to figure out what she could give up so she wouldn't have to give him up.

He moved his hands to her arms then, gently running his palms from her biceps down to her wrists. "Your sleeve was ripped. Do you have bruises? Anything feel like it's broken? I should have taken you to the ER to get checked—"

She pressed her fingers over his lips to stop him. "I feel fine. Physically..." That wasn't entirely true, though; she did have bruises and she was sore. "It's just that this feels so unreal, what happened, you being here, it's like a dream..."

"Or a nightmare?" he asked, arching one dark eyebrow.

She'd had both about him. Nightmares where he

found out about the twins and was so furious that he threatened to take them away from her because of her being so cruel to keep them apart for so many years. And dreams that he'd been with them the entire time…

"We need to talk about the girls," she said.

"About telling them that I'm their father?"

She nodded. "I don't want to tell them if you don't want anything to do with them. I don't want them to get hurt…" Her voice cracked on that last word with the pain she'd felt when their marriage had ended.

He flinched and closed his eyes as if he was feeling that pain, too. "I don't want that either," he said.

"What do you want?" she asked. "Do you want to be part of their lives? And how would that look? How much time can you give them? More than you gave to us?"

He sucked in a breath as if she'd punched him. And as he stepped back, a door opened and a little girl shrieked.

Ana ran into the hallway, screaming while Luci chased after her, yelling, "Bang. Bang." And she pointed her index finger while pulling back her thumb as if she was pulling a trigger, as if she was shooting her sister.

Brennan had called an informal meeting instead of an official one since the FBI director, Roberta Chang, was out of town at a conference. She'd considered canceling her appearance at the conference because of the Landmark Killer, but Brennan and the rest of the team had insisted they had it under control.

But they didn't.

Bodies kept turning up. And the notes...

Not just the ones in the pockets of the victims, but the ones texted to him and to Cash. Where was Cash?

Brennan looked around the conference room he'd commandeered for the meeting. But only his sister Ashlynn, brother Patrick and the director's assistant, Xander Washer, were in the room. Ashlynn and Patrick were standing near the entrance, like they were half out the door, while Xander sat in a chair, a pen in his hand as if he was going to take notes for them.

Or more likely taking notes for his boss, who undoubtedly had told the young man to keep her apprised of the investigation. Hell, at the moment, Xander probably knew more about what was going on than he did.

"Where's Cash?" Brennan asked uneasily. Fraternal twins, they didn't quite have that twin-tuition thing where they knew when each other was in danger or anything. But with a serial killer taunting them, it wasn't much of a stretch to think that something might have happened to Cash.

"You didn't hear?" Ashlynn asked.

"About what?"

"Someone nearly ran down Valentina yesterday."

Brennan cursed. He didn't need twin tuition to know how much Cash loved his ex-wife, even now, years after their divorce. "Is she all right?"

Ashlynn nodded. "Yes, Cash was there and saved

her. And the car that was used was tracked down last night. It had been stolen right before the attempt."

"And afterward, it was burned," Patrick added. He was the co-head of the FBI crime scene investigation division. "We went over it. No DNA, no prints. No evidence to figure out who stole it."

"Nothing?" Brennan asked, his stomach sinking at the thought of someone else being out there, trying to take out another Colton.

Patrick shook his head. "No evidence, but from the distance between the seat and steering wheel, we can conclude that the last person who drove it was probably close to six feet tall."

Xander's pen moved across the page.

"You probably don't need to take notes about this," Brennan said. "I doubt it has anything to do with the Landmark Killer."

"Why not?" Xander asked. "Didn't Cash get a note about his ex?"

"A text," Ashlynn corrected him. "But this isn't the Landmark Killer's MO. He doesn't use vehicles or go after women and kids."

"Kids?" Brennan asked.

Ashlynn nodded. "Yes, Valentina has twin girls."

"How old?"

"Old enough that I heard them talking while he was on the phone with me," Ashlynn said. "But I don't know anything about kids."

Something about her tone, and the way that she looked away as if unwilling to meet his gaze, had Brennan wondering if she knew more.

"If they were talking," Xander said, "they must be at least a couple years old."

Either Valentina had moved on quickly, while Cash hadn't moved on at all, or…

Those kids were his.

No wonder Cash hadn't shown up at the office today. He'd put work before his marriage and lost his wife three years ago. If those kids were his, he'd probably do whatever he could to make sure he didn't lose them, too.

To a killer, like they'd lost their dad.

But Brennan wondered if it had really been the Landmark Killer going after Valentina. Or someone else, like the person who'd gone after Stella recently.

Did Valentina have an enemy? A stalker? Someone obsessed with her besides Cash?

Chapter 9

"No bang, no bang!" Ana cried, tears streaking down her face.

Cash bent over to pick her up, but before he could reach for her, Valentina pushed him aside and picked up the toddler herself. Didn't she think he was capable of comforting a crying child?

"Your holster," she whispered at him. "They must have seen your weapon."

He'd made a point of keeping his shirt over it, but maybe when they'd been washing dishes, they'd caught a glimpse of it, especially when they were spraying water at him. He didn't know if they'd noticed it, but with as bright and observant as they were, they probably had. Or maybe they remembered him drawing it in the street and shooting at that car if they'd been able to see that from their stroller.

Since he couldn't comfort Ana, he reached for Luci instead, catching her shoulders and stopping her from mock-shooting her sister, who was clearly terrified. "Hey, no bang bang here," he said.

He and his siblings hadn't even played cops and robbers growing up like other kids had because, as the kids of an officer, they'd known how serious crime and how dangerous guns really were. Knowing that, they'd all wanted to be in law enforcement, like their dad, even then. And after his death, they'd been even more determined, which had probably broken their mother's heart.

Celeste Colton never said that, though, had never discouraged them from their careers. But maybe that was why she'd moved to Florida some years ago, to remove herself from the front-row seat to their dangerous professions. News of the Landmark Killer had probably made it to West Palm Beach, though, and if not through the media, then through one of his siblings' weekly calls to her.

He would have a lot to tell her on his next call. That is, if he could convince Valentina to let him tell the girls first that he was their father. But now she blamed him for their violent playing.

"Pretending to shoot someone is not a good game to play," he told Luci.

But the little girl stared up at him with a blank expression in her green eyes. She clearly had no idea what he was talking about. And she was too young for him to try to explain.

"You scared your sister," he pointed out, hoping that would get through to her.

"Bang bang," she said. "The bad man go bang bang."

The bad man hadn't shot at them, though. He'd driven a car at them. "Did you see that on TV?" he asked. "Is that what you're talking about?"

She shook her head, tumbling curls around her face.

"I don't let them watch shows like that," Valentina said, her voice sharp as if she was offended that he would think she had.

"Even cartoons are violent nowadays," he said, which was one of the many reasons he'd given her for why he hadn't wanted to bring children into the world. It was too full of violence.

But she'd countered that was why good was necessary, to counteract the bad. If only that was how it worked...

"They must have seen your weapon," she insisted. "When you shot at the car."

That had all happened so quickly that Cash couldn't recall where everyone had been and what they might have seen. His focus had been on stopping that vehicle from hitting them.

"Am I the bad man then?" he asked. He certainly had been in their marriage, the one who'd denied her what she'd wanted. His time and a family.

Luci reached up and touched his face. "The fib..."

He was so much more, but now he worried that
Valentina might never let him tell them. Of course
that didn't mean he couldn't tell them himself. But
he didn't want to upset her either, especially when
she had valid concerns that he might disappoint and
hurt them. He was concerned about that, too, with
that sick feeling in his gut again.

"You two are soaked," Valentina remarked.

Three, if she'd included him.

"You were supposed to wash the dishes, not your-
selves," she said. "Go back to your rooms and change
into dry clothes. Then bring me your wet pajamas
and I'll put them in the dryer." She set Ana on her
feet and she and Luci ran back into their room, their
earlier scuffle forgotten.

By them...

It was clear from the tension gripping Valentina
and the line between her eyebrows that she was worried.

"I didn't show them the gun," he said quietly. But
he couldn't swear that they hadn't seen it, and she
knew that as well.

"I don't want them getting hurt," she said, and
she stepped into her bedroom and gestured for him
to follow her. She probably didn't want the girls to
overhear this conversation.

Because she didn't want them to hear any more
about the gun? Or about his being their father?

"By whoever tried running them and you over or
by me?" he asked.

"Both," she said.

"I don't either," he said. "But I feel like they should know who I am to them. Something I should have known before this, too."

Her face flushed, and she dropped her gaze down to her hands, which she twisted together now that she wasn't holding their daughter. "I know."

He hadn't expected her to admit that.

"But you told me you didn't want kids," she reminded him. "So I didn't think you would want to know, that you would want to be responsible for something you never wanted…"

A pang struck his heart; it hurt him that she'd thought he would reject his kids. That he wouldn't want them.

Because even though he didn't know them, he was falling for them as hard and quickly as he'd fallen for their mother when he'd met her. He'd loved her so much that he'd ignored the decisions he'd made so long ago about never getting married and focusing only on his career. But when she'd been unhappy with him being gone so much and missing holidays and anniversaries and canceling planned vacations, he'd known he'd made a mistake.

That he'd been selfish then. Was it selfish now to want the girls to know he was their father if he couldn't figure out how to give more of himself to them than he had their mother?

Valentina held her breath as she waited for Cash to say something, anything to indicate that he wanted to be a father to their daughters. That he didn't regret her having them. That he could love them like she loved them.

Like she'd once loved him. Because she'd loved him, she hadn't wanted to hurt him just as she didn't want him hurting the girls. But she had, by keeping the girls from him and how she'd just reacted.

"I'm sorry," she said. "I should have told you the minute I learned I was pregnant." She had a lot of excuses why she hadn't; excuses she'd already given him to justify what she'd done. She'd been giving herself those same excuses the past three years, but she knew she'd acted selfishly.

He didn't say anything, didn't acknowledge her apology at all.

She knew it wasn't enough to make up for the years of their daughters' lives that he'd missed. She would never be able to compensate for that, and guilt swirled around her stomach with all the coffee she'd drunk to wake up after she'd spent the night before reeling from everything that had happened.

"And I shouldn't have blamed you for the bang-bang thing," she added. "They could have picked up something at day care. Anywhere, really..."

He continued to just stare at her, as if not following what she was saying. And that unnerved her. That stare. And how his wet shirt molded to his chest.

Nerves and attraction getting to her, she continued to ramble out more apologies. "And I'm sorry that I haven't let you change and put your shirt in the dryer—"

As she had earlier, he pressed a finger to her lips. "Shh, it's okay."

She had a feeling that he wasn't talking about everything she'd done and had just apologized for doing. Probably just the shirt…

Especially when he stepped back and shrugged off the one he wore over the wet T-shirt. Then with a glance at the door, he quickly took off his holster and reached above her armoire, setting it atop there and well out of the reach of the little girls. Then he lifted his T-shirt over his washboard abs and then over his chest.

Valentina's pulse raced as her skin heated. She'd never wanted anyone the way she'd wanted him. He was so sexy, with lean muscles lightly dusted with dark hair. Soft hair…

Hair that had tickled her skin when she'd lain in his arms, her body against his body. Touching everywhere…

She wanted to touch him again like that, wanted to be close to him, wanted to kiss him.

And maybe he saw that desire on her face, because he stepped close to her again. Almost involuntarily, she reached for him, sliding her hands over his chest like she had so many times before. She loved how the soft hair tickled her skin.

He leaned down, his head close to hers, and she rose up on tiptoe just enough that her mouth brushed across his. He wrapped his arms around her, pulling her closer as he kissed her back, deeply, passionately.

He tasted sweet, like the syrup from the pancakes,

but he acted like he was hungry yet, like he couldn't get enough of her mouth, of her kisses.

And she kept kissing him as she ran her hands over his chest. His heart beat hard and fast beneath her palm. And he panted for breath, like she panted.

"Mommy!"

Startled, she jerked away as Cash stepped back. And they both whirled toward the doorway where two little girls stood, staring at them in shock. They'd never seen her kissing anyone before.

She hadn't dated since the divorce; hadn't found anyone that sparked her interest enough.

Because no one could ever be their father.

He stared down at the gun that he held in his gloved hand, the gun that had taken so many lives. He needed another gun. One that couldn't be traced to other crimes.

So many other crimes…

He'd gotten sloppy.

Complacent.

That was what had gone wrong yesterday.

It had gotten too easy for him to kill. And he'd begun to take it for granted that he would never be caught. That there was no way anyone could identify him. But that had been before yesterday.

Before…

He couldn't miss again. And with a gun, he had a far better track record than he had with a car. That had been so damn sloppy yesterday; he was lucky he hadn't gotten caught or shot then.

With the gun, he wouldn't miss the next time. He just had to wait for another chance to present itself. And he wasn't sure when that would be…

When they would be as vulnerable as they'd been yesterday.

But eventually, if he watched and waited, the moment would come, and he would be ready. He would make certain that he ended it this time. And that there would be no way to trace any of his crimes back to him.

And nobody around to identify him.

Chapter 10

Cash's body went from hot to cold. One minute he was burning up with desire for Valentina, his skin on fire wherever she touched him, and the next...

"Mommy!"

The word hit him like a bucket of ice. And it must have hit her just as hard because she jumped back, away from him, as if he was the one who'd thrown the cold water on her.

The girls looked just as stunned as they stared at him from the doorway, their eyes wide. He grabbed his button-down shirt and thrust his arms in the sleeves. Clearly they weren't used to seeing their mother kissing shirtless men. That tension inside him eased some, but then he felt a pang of guilt as well.

He'd divorced her so she could move on and be

happy. So she would find the happiness she deserved. The family she'd wanted...

He hadn't figured on her being a single mother; he knew how hard that had been on his mom after his dad's murder. And he hadn't wanted that for Valentina. Even if he'd agreed to try for the children she'd wanted, he'd known that with the time his job took that she would have essentially been raising them on her own.

Like she'd wound up doing anyway.

He should have hoped for her to have someone in her life to take care of her for once instead of her taking care of everyone else. But selfishly, he wanted her, and if the little girls hadn't come to find their mommy, he wasn't sure what would have happened between them.

"Mommy? Why you kiss fib?" Luci asked the question.

And Cash nearly groaned at the name his children called him. He knew they meant FBI agent, but to him, it just sounded like fib, like a lie, for so many reasons. For one, he didn't even feel like much of an FBI agent since he had no idea who the Landmark Killer was, and for another, because of his hunt for the serial killer, he had put Valentina and the girls in danger. And for another, he hadn't even noticed them sneaking up on him because he'd been so distracted kissing their mother.

What if the killer had gotten into the condo?

What if it had been him instead of them?

He had to be more careful. He had to ignore the

attraction he'd always had for Valentina. No. It was more than attraction. So much more…

Valentina drew in a deep breath before smiling, albeit a little too brightly, at their daughters. She stepped back and settled onto the edge of her bed, then she patted the places on both sides of her and said, "Come here. I need to tell you who this really is."

And Cash's heart kicked back into the high gear it had been in during their kiss. But this was different. That had been passion; this was panic. He'd been bugging her to tell them, but now…

The little girls climbed onto the bed next to their mother, and she scooted them around until they all sat against the profusion of colorful pillows she'd always liked to have on the bed.

"What, Mommy?" Luci asked with curiosity. "He not the fib?" She pointed a small hand at him, and her green eyes, so like his, narrowed with a trace of suspicion.

"He is an FBI agent," Valentina said. "He catches bad people and puts them in jail."

"Bang bang bad guys?" Ana asked, her voice a bit squeaky and shaky.

"I don't shoot them," Cash assured her with a glance up at where he'd concealed his weapon from them. He couldn't understand their fascination with guns. He was more uncomfortable with that than the lie he'd just told them; he had had to use his weapon in the past. But he didn't want them to think he killed people. "I don't want anyone to get hurt," he said. "Especially good people."

"Sparky," Ana murmured. "Sparky…"

Cash looked at Valentina, trying to understand what the little girl meant, but she raised her shoulders in a shrug, then pointed at the window. "The sun's a little bright. Maybe that's it…"

Cash stepped in front of the window, blocking some of that light, casting a shadow over the bed where the people he wanted most to protect were cuddled together. And it was as if that beam of sunshine pierced through his heart now, warming it.

Valentina looked cold, though, as if she pulled the little girls closer for warmth or comfort. "I should have talked to you two about this a while ago. I should have talked to…" She glanced up then and met his gaze, and tears glistened in her dark eyes. "But I didn't know how to tell you…"

Luci reached up then and touched her mother's cheek. "What, Mommy?"

"You know how some kids at day care have daddies that come pick them up?" she asked.

Ana nodded.

"We don't have a daddy," Luci said.

Now pain pierced Cash's heart.

"You do have a daddy," Valentina said. "This is your daddy." And like Luci had, she pointed at him, and her hand was shaking.

The girls followed the direction of her index finger to him. And their eyes widened.

"The fib?" Luci asked.

"Daddy," Ana murmured, and tears glistened in her eyes as if she was moved that she could use that name.

And tears stung Cash's eyes that she'd used it for him. That he was a daddy...

"Daddy!" Luci said it, too, with conviction, and then she jumped up and ran across the bed toward him, vaulting into his arms.

He caught her and held her close. And then Ana was there, too, tentatively, shyly, following her twin across the bed. She stood behind Luci, waiting.

He reached for her, too, with his other arm, folding her against him, holding them both. He'd had no intention of ever becoming a father, but now that he was, he couldn't imagine these little girls not being in the world. He had to do his best to protect them. To keep them safe. But he knew that he didn't have to protect them just from bad men; he had to protect them from himself.

Valentina couldn't get over the sense of panic that had been pressing down on her chest since that morning when she'd told the girls that Cash was their father. No. She'd been panicking even before that, when she'd kissed Cash. When she'd wanted him so badly that they would probably have made love if the girls hadn't interrupted them when they had.

Well, for her it would have been making love. She wasn't sure what it would have been for him. She struggled to believe that he loved her, that he'd ever loved her, or he wouldn't have served her with divorce papers so quickly. He would have tried to find a way to meet her halfway.

But then she wasn't sure what that would have been. What was the compromise between having a family and not having one? She couldn't imagine not having the girls in her life.

Even now she could hear them giggling as they played in their room. And the deep rumble of Cash's voice as he played with them.

And that panic pressed harder, squeezing her heart. She couldn't fall for him again. She couldn't.

Because nothing had changed. He was still all about his job. And she knew why…

She'd always known. She pulled the *New York Wire* from the drawer of her bedside table. The article told everyone else the story of how a serial killer had murdered his father, leading to Cash and his siblings dedicating their lives to catching and stopping other serial killers.

His crusade was admirable, one of the many reasons she'd fallen in love with him. She hadn't wanted him to stop, just to give her some of his time and energy as well. And to give her the family she'd wanted…

She had that now. At least she had her girls. She doubted she would ever have Cash, but now that he knew he was a father, she hoped he would make an effort with them. That was why she'd decided to tell them, and so that they would stop calling him the fib.

She'd kept the truth too long from everyone. Even herself.

She'd known she needed to do this, to tell them. Her parents had urged her to do it, had even threatened to tell Cash for her. But she'd insisted that she was doing the right thing for all of them. And she'd thought she was right.

Until the girls had called him Daddy…

Tears stung her eyes, and she blinked furiously.

"Are you okay?" a deep voice asked.

And she turned to find Cash leaning against the doorjamb, staring at her. Usually she would have sensed his presence. She would have reacted as she did now, with an increased pulse and tingling skin. She'd wanted him so badly earlier when his mouth had moved over hers, when her hands had moved over his naked chest.

She still wanted him that badly, so badly that her hands shook on the newspaper when she tried to put it back into the open drawer.

He stepped forward and took it from her, his handsome face twisting into a grimace of disgust and frustration.

"Stella Maxwell knows you well," she remarked, trying to ignore the little sting of jealousy she felt.

Cash grinned. "Not me. Brennan. They're together now."

"I'm glad he has someone," she said. She had always liked Cash's twin, so much so that she didn't like how that reporter had betrayed Brennan's trust for a story. "But that article…"

"Stella didn't write it," Cash said. "Well, maybe she did write some of it, but she didn't submit it to her editor to print. She wouldn't have done that to Brennan. Somebody hacked her computer and added to the article, then submitted it to her editor."

"Somebody?"

"Either a mole in Stella's office or the Landmark Killer," he said with a glance over his shoulder as if checking to make sure the twins hadn't sneaked up on them again.

"You think he could have been behind that, too?"

He nodded. "He's been messing with Brennan and me, and he sent a text to our cousin Sinead, too."

"The FBI profiler?"

He nodded. "Whoever it is, he knows everybody working the case. He knows how to get a hold of us without the texts getting traced back to him."

She shivered.

"I'm sorry," he said. "I never wanted this part of my life to touch you, to affect you, and I definitely never wanted to put you in danger." He glanced toward the doorway again. "Or them…"

"Did they fall asleep?" she asked. She hadn't heard any giggling or movement since she'd noticed him in the doorway.

He nodded, a small smile curving his mouth. "They were playing so hard, and then they just crashed into their beds. At first I thought they were pretending they'd fallen asleep, but they're out."

She smiled. "They usually take a nap about this time of the afternoon."

His smile slipped down into a frown. "I don't

know anything about them. Their schedules. When they took their first steps, their first word…"

Mama. But she wasn't about to share that with him. "I'm sorry," she said. "I really thought I was doing the right thing, that you didn't want…"

He nodded.

But then she let out a soft curse, at herself. "But I was really just doing what was easiest for me."

"Raising twins all by yourself?" he asked. "That was easiest?"

"Easier than seeing you again," she admitted.

And he flinched. "I didn't realize you hated me that much."

It was just the opposite, but she couldn't admit it without revealing that she still had feelings for him. Feelings that she knew would only lead her back to the same heartbreak she'd felt before.

But she couldn't let him think she hated him, so she shook her head. "It wasn't that," she assured him. "It was just easier to have a clean break. You must have thought the same, because you had those divorce papers served to me so quickly after I moved out. I got them before I even realized I was pregnant."

She'd thought it was just stress over the separation that had made her so sick after she'd moved into her grandparents' condo. She'd been using an IUD as birth control, so she hadn't considered that she could actually be pregnant.

"I thought it would be easier that way," he said. "I was so focused on the case at the time, and I kept disappointing you…" He glanced toward that open doorway, and she knew he was worried about the same thing she was, that he would disappoint them as well.

"The longer you stay here, the more attached they will get to you," she warned him. But she was worried that they weren't the only ones who would get used to him being here.

"I have to stay," he said. "I have to make sure nothing happens to any of you."

She knew they'd had a very close call the day before, and without Cash there to save them, they might not have survived it. But she'd had a close call just a short while ago…with him.

With kissing him, with wanting him…

His staying here was bad enough, but if she let him back into her bed as well as her life, she wasn't sure she would be able to let him go again. She wasn't sure that she would want to.

So she drew in a deep breath and braced herself to resist the temptation he'd always posed for her. She could not touch him again. Or kiss him.

Or even look at him too long like she was looking at him now standing in the doorway. So tall. So intense. His gaze was focused on her with that look in his green eyes again, that heat.

She jumped up from the bed, knowing that she had to get out of it before she did something stupid, like pull him into it with her.

"I have baby books for them," she said. "They're on the shelves by the TV. There are DVDs, too, of them. They love getting their pictures taken and having me record them." But as much of their lives as she could show him, he hadn't been there in the moment. He hadn't shared the experience with them. But would he have, even if he'd known about them? Or would work have consumed him then as it always had?

And probably still did…

His phone vibrated with an incoming text. His hand shook a bit as he pulled it from his pocket; maybe he was worried that it was another one from the Landmark Killer. Another taunt…

Whatever it was, it drew his attention away from her. And she was happy for that this time. Because if he'd kept looking at her the way he'd been, she wasn't sure how long she would have been able to resist temptation.

Chapter 11

A week had passed since Cash moved into the condo. A week he'd taken off work, which was unprecedented for him. A week he'd asked Valentina to take off from the library as well, and to keep the girls home from day care.

He could keep them safe here.

He was the only one in danger in the condo.

Danger of getting used to this, to living in the sun-filled home with the view he was appreciating at the moment, as he stood in front of the windows staring at the Cyclone roller coaster and the Ferris wheel at Luna Park. Beyond the rides, the water glistened in the morning sunshine.

Even more than the place, he was getting used to the people who lived here. His family. While Valentina was his ex-wife, she would always be the mother of his children. Always be part of his life now...

And she would always hold a part of his heart, if not the whole thing. No. The little girls had taken the rest of it. Every minute with them, every smile and giggle and hug, had love overwhelming him. The love he felt for them...

And the love he thought they were beginning to feel for him. They were getting attached to him, just as Valentina must have been worrying about. They were getting used to him being part of their every-day lives.

They'd watched all the DVDs with him that Valentina had taken to document every one of their milestones. Part of him hoped she'd been documenting them for him as much as for herself. That she had intended to show them to him one day. The girls showed him their baby books and photo albums themselves. And they'd taught him how to play Chutes and Ladders and Hungry Hungry Hippos and all the other board games they'd been playing over the last week. They'd also watched a ton of movies and cartoons, with their mother letting them stay up past their bedtime more often than not.

He wondered about that. Had she done it because they were excited about him being there and she hadn't wanted to limit their time with him? Or had she done it because she'd wanted to limit her time alone with him?

Once the kids went to bed at night, she slipped off to her room shortly after, closing the door in his face, closing him out. But despite that, they'd talked about their lives over the past three years.

About his job and his family. And about her job and her family.

They'd even talked about how crazy the world had gotten with polarizing politics and inflation and all the things that ordinary married couples probably discussed. They'd never talked that much when they'd been married, though.

The nights he'd been home from his job, they had spent in bed together, and they'd done very little talking at all then, making up for the time they'd been apart. His body ached to make up with her that way, for all the lost years. He wanted her so damn badly. Wanted to kiss her again and hold her and join their bodies together the way they used to, where he'd felt like he was coming home.

Like she was his home. Not an apartment or a condo, but her. He'd never felt as though he'd belonged anywhere as much as he'd belonged in her arms.

"They fell asleep," Valentina remarked as she joined him in the living room. She seemed nervous, on edge.

He was, too, had been since that kiss. Sleeping on the couch, so close but yet so far from Valentina, was killing him. He wanted—no, he needed—to be back in her bed, back in her arms and she in his. He ached for her.

"Is that bad that they fell asleep?" he asked.

Maybe she was worried what would happen if

they were alone together too long, if she would kiss him again, like she had that day, like he'd wanted her to kiss him and touch him again ever since.

"It's morning," she said. "They never take a nap this early in the day."

"They get up at the crack of dawn," he said with a smile.

"Like you," she murmured.

They were like him in some ways, ways he wouldn't have expected since he hadn't lived with them until this week, until now. The early rising, the things they liked to eat, the shows they liked were even some of the old cartoons he'd watched as a kid, the Disney movies he'd loved when life had still been innocent and simple for him.

When his dad had been alive...

But when his dad had died, Cash's innocence and optimism had died with him. He'd known then how much evil there was in the world, how innocent people could be killed for no reason.

Like whoever had tried to kill Valentina and the girls when he'd aimed that car at them, not once but twice. That hadn't been an accident, especially not when the stolen car had been set on fire just a short while later. Ashlynn and Patrick thinking it was the work of a professional made him even more determined to stay here, to keep them safe.

But what motive would anyone have to want to hurt those sweet girls and their mother? Besides the Landmark Killer messing with Cash?

"I need to go back to work," she said. "And they

"One Minute" Survey

You get up to **FOUR books**
<u>and</u> a Mystery Gift...

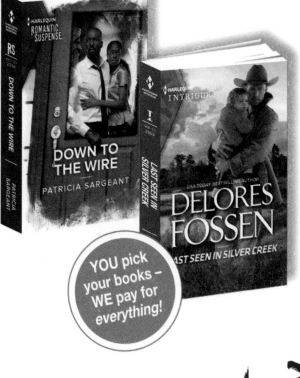

YOU pick your books –
WE pay for everything.
You get up to FOUR new books and a Mystery Gift…
absolutely FREE!
Total retail value: Over $20!

Dear Reader,

Your opinions are important to us. So if you'll participate in our fast and free "One Minute" Survey, YOU can pick up to four wonderful books that WE pay for when you try the Harlequin Reader Service!

As a leading publisher of women's fiction, we'd love to hear from you. That's why we promise to reward you for completing our survey.

IMPORTANT: Please complete the survey and return it. We'll send your Free Books and a Free Mystery Gift right away. And we pay for shipping and handling too! *We pay for EVERYTHING!*

Try **Harlequin® Romantic Suspense** and get 2 books featuring heart-racing page-turners with unexpected plot twists and irresistible chemistry that will keep you guessing to the very end.

Try **Harlequin Intrigue® Larger-Print** and get 2 books featuring action-packed stories that will keep you on the edge of your seat. Solve the crime and deliver justice at all costs.

Or TRY BOTH!

Thank you again for participating in our "One Minute" Survey. It really takes just a minute (or less) to complete the survey… and your free books and gift will be well worth it!

If you continue with your subscription, you can look forward to curated monthly shipments of brand-new books from your selected series, always at a discount off the cover price! Plus you can cancel any time. So don't miss out, return your One Minute Survey today to get your Free books.

Pam Powers

"One Minute" Survey

GET YOUR FREE BOOKS AND A FREE GIFT!

✓ Complete this Survey   ✓ Return this survey

◀ **DETACH AND MAIL CARD TODAY!** ▶

1 Do you try to find time to read every day?

☐ YES   ☐ NO

2 Do you prefer stories with suspensful storylines?

☐ YES   ☐ NO

3 Do you enjoy having books delivered to your home?

☐ YES   ☐ NO

4 Do you share your favorite books with friends?

☐ YES   ☐ NO

YES! I have completed the above "One Minute" Survey. Please send me my Free Books and a Free Mystery Gift (worth over $20 retail). I understand that I am under no obligation to buy anything, as explained on the back of this card.

☐ **Harlequin® Romantic Suspense** 240/340 CTI G2AD

☐ **Harlequin Intrigue® Larger-Print** 199/399 CTI G2AD

☐ **BOTH** 240/340 & 199/399 CTI G2AE

FIRST NAME   LAST NAME

ADDRESS

APT.#   CITY

STATE/PROV.   ZIP/POSTAL CODE

EMAIL ☐ Please check this box if you would like to receive newsletters and promotional emails from Harlequin Enterprises ULC and its affiliates. You can unsubscribe anytime.

© 2023 HARLEQUIN ENTERPRISES ULC
™ and ® are trademarks owned by Harlequin Enterprises ULC. Printed in the U.S.A.

HI/HRS-1123-OM

need to go back to day care, back to their usual schedule." The desperation was in her voice and in the dark circles beneath her eyes. She didn't appear to be sleeping any better in her bed than he was on the couch.

If only…

He started toward her then, wanting to kiss her again as they'd kissed that day. Wanting to be with her.

But he'd only taken a couple of steps before his cell rang and vibrated in his pocket. So it wouldn't wake up the twins, he grabbed it quickly, and instead of rejecting the call as he'd intended, he accidentally accepted it. Maybe because his hand was shaking from the desire for Valentina that was coursing through him.

"Cash?" Brennan's voice emanated from the cell speaker.

"I'll give you privacy," Valentina said, and she darted back into the hall as if she'd been looking for an excuse to escape from him, as if she'd known what he'd been about to do. To kiss her…

"Cash?" Brennan called out again.

"I'm here," he said, and he took the phone off speaker so that the sound of their uncle's voice wouldn't wake up the girls.

It was early for them to fall asleep, though they'd all stayed up a little late last night, eating popcorn and watching *Aladdin*. Then they'd wanted to have a slumber party in the living room with him, but Valentina had insisted that the couch was too small for all of them.

He could have suggested that they move the slumber party to her bedroom, to her big king-size bed. But he hadn't wanted to put her on the spot like that, and he wasn't certain he could share a bed with her and not want more.

It was probably good that Brennan had called when he had, so that Cash hadn't kissed her again. He wouldn't have been able to stop at just a kiss.

But he released a ragged sigh, of disappointment, before asking, "What's up?"

"You tell me," Brennan said. "I haven't seen you all week."

"You know why," he reminded him. He'd let Brennan know that he had to work remotely for the time being instead of going into the office. Not that he'd really been doing much working on anything but catching up on his daughters' lives and all of it he'd missed. "I can't let anything happen to Valentina or the girls…"

"You can have Dave Percell keep an eye on them for you like he did the week after you received that text."

"That was just a text," Cash said. "That wasn't a car trying to run them down."

"You don't know that that had anything to do with the Landmark Killer," Brennan pointed out. "In fact I'm pretty damn sure that it didn't. His victims have all been blond, blue-eyed men in their thirties."

"He's going after us, too," Cash reminded him. "With those taunting texts, with that article in the *New York Wire*. He's messing with us, and if it wasn't him that was driving that car, it might have been someone he hired."

Brennan sucked in a breath. "I hadn't considered that. From Sinead's profile of him, it seems like he would be someone who'd work alone."

"He works with us," Cash said.

Brennan cursed. "We need to figure out who. We've got to stop him. So I called a meeting for this afternoon, and you need to be there, too, Cash. We can't meet here because that damn Landmark Killer would know about it, would know that we're onto him, so I called it outside the office. Because you need to be there, I booked a hotel room not that far from where you're staying."

"Ah…" He appreciated that Brennan had considered him when he'd chosen the location. But he was torn. Getting out of the condo for a moment, getting some distance between him and Valentina, might clear his head and protect his heart.

But…

"I called Dave Percell, too," Brennan said. "He's on his way over to watch the door for you."

"That didn't go that well last time," he said. "Her neighbor got all uptight about it and was saying that the condo board wouldn't approve of her being here if it put other residents in danger." Of course he'd probably been saying all that out of spite, because he'd been hitting on Valentina. Blake Highland wouldn't do that anymore if he knew what was good for him.

"You need to be here, Cash. We need to stop this

guy before he claims another victim. And if he hired someone to go after Valentina and the girls, that would stop that, too," Brennan said. "That would make them safer than your playing house is making them."

Cash flinched. Playing house. Was that all he was doing?

"And if he's not behind that attempt on their lives, you need to figure out who is."

"What are you saying?"

"You could have other enemies. With our job, we've all made enemies," Brennan pointed out. "Hell, anybody can make an enemy, some without even realizing it. Like Stella. That attempt on the lives of Valentina and the girls might have to do with something else. Even with Valentina…"

Cash snorted at the thought of her making an enemy. "Stella is a reporter. Valentina is a librarian. She doesn't make enemies."

"Maybe someone really doesn't like being shushed," Brennan joked.

But Cash couldn't laugh about someone going after his family. His brother was right, though. The best way to keep them safe was to figure out who was behind the threat and the attempt on their lives and stop them.

"Okay, I'll be there," he said. He could trust Dave to protect them like he had that first night, making sure that the predatory neighbor hadn't been able to even speak to Valentina until Cash had had her open the door.

Just how predatory was the guy? And how angry that Valentina kept rebuffing his advances? Angry enough to try to kill her?

Cash shook his head at the ridiculous thought, at the idea that Brennan had planted in his mind that the person who was after Valentina and the girls was someone in her life, someone she knew, who wanted to hurt her.

Shortly after he'd taken that call, Cash was gone. Valentina should have been relieved to get a break from him and the feelings that kept overwhelming her in his presence. Guilt and regret that she hadn't told him about their daughters sooner, that intensified every time she watched him with them. With every hug they gave him, she thought of all the other hugs she'd denied him.

But she couldn't know how many he would have had, how much he would have been around them if he'd known about them when she was pregnant. He might not have been there for her or them then. He was only here now because of that text and his saving them from someone trying to run them down.

But guilt and regret weren't even the most overwhelming feelings she had. Desire was. She wanted him so badly. Maybe it was just because she'd denied that part of her life for so long, that she'd pushed aside her needs as a woman and had totally focused on being a mother.

She didn't feel much like a mom at the moment, though, because she wasn't protecting her kids from the heartbreak that was sure to come. The heartbreak that Cash would inevitably cause them, just like he'd caused her, when he'd been unable to give her the time and attention she'd needed from him. Which hadn't been much...

Little kids needed more.

And now the guilt surged back because Valentina realized she hadn't checked on them lately. They'd been napping for a while and at a time when they usually wouldn't have napped at all. Concerned, she hurried from her bedroom to theirs.

Ana sat up in her bed, flipping through the pages of one of her picture books, while Luci was huddled under the covers in hers. "Shh, Mommy," Ana said. "Luci seepy."

Valentina dropped to her knees between their beds. "She's been sleeping for a long time."

"Long time," Ana agreed.

"It was sweet of you to let her sleep," she praised her daughter. But it had been neglectful on Valentina's part; she should have checked on the girls earlier. She reached out now to do so, pulling back the blanket to touch Luci's forehead. It was damp and hot, like the hair plastered to her head. She was burning up.

Luci shivered, her bottom lip quivering. "Sooo cold..." she murmured, and she grabbed at the blanket to pull it over her head again.

"Oh, baby." Panic gripped Valentina, but she forced herself to appear calm as she hurried to the medicine cabinet in her bathroom and grabbed a thermometer and the bottle of children's pain and fever relief.

She had to pull back the blanket again to get a reading with the forehead thermometer. And she swallowed her gasp of alarm over how high it was.

"Come on, Luci," she said. "You need to take some medicine." She poured the recommended dosage into the liquid medicine dispenser and pressed it to the little girl's lips, which were already starting to crack. Once she got Luci awake enough to swallow the medicine, she hurried to put that bottle away before getting some Pedialyte from the refrigerator. The poor little girl was already getting dehydrated. Valentina got her to drink some of that before Luci fell asleep again.

Then, shaky with fear for her sick child, Valentina ducked back into her own bedroom to call the girls' pediatrician's office.

"If her fever doesn't come down, you need to bring her into the office," the nurse advised.

Cash had been insistent that they didn't leave the condo. He'd even told his friend as much when Sergeant Percell had shown up to guard the door.

But if Luci's fever didn't go down, it was going to be more dangerous for the little girl inside the condo than it would be to make the short trip to the doctor's office, especially since there had been no more threats or attempts on their lives.

Maybe the whole thing with the car had just been a warning for Cash to back off. And since he'd stayed with them the past week, he had. So maybe there was

no more threat to them but the fever that was currently ravaging poor Luci.

If her fever didn't go down soon, there was no
way that officer or Cash or anyone else, even a serial
killer, was going to prevent Valentina from getting
her daughter the medical help she needed.

Chapter 12

Ever since he'd left the condo, Cash had been on edge. Hell, he'd been on edge even before he'd left. He'd been on edge since he'd received that anonymous text about his murdered daddy and his sad ex-wife.

Staying with Valentina and the girls the past week had nearly pushed him over that edge. He'd wanted to do more than protect her; he'd wanted to be with her, with all the passion that had always burned so hot between them. But that would have been dangerous for both of them. He couldn't afford any distractions right now, and neither could she and the girls. He had to keep them safe.

Dave had promised he'd make sure they didn't leave the condo and that nobody got inside, but he was just one man. What if more than one person came after them or...

"You're here, but you're not here," Brennan commented from where he sat at the desk in the hotel suite he'd booked for the meeting.

Cash knew who his twin was talking about and released a ragged sigh, and suddenly he was so weary, he considered lying back on the bed where he was sitting to close his eyes. "I'm sorry. I know I haven't been doing my part in catching this psychopath."

"You've been busy," Ashlynn said sympathetically, "with Valentina and the girls..."

She trailed off, and he knew what she was asking, what, knowing his sister, she'd probably already investigated to find out.

To confirm what everyone else either knew or at least suspected, Cash said, "Valentina's daughters, Ana and Luciana, are mine."

Predictably, nobody looked surprised. They were concerned and maybe confused, though, as they stared at him with sympathetic expressions on their faces.

"I can't believe Valentina didn't tell you about them," Ashlynn said.

"She didn't think I wanted to be a father," Cash said in her defense.

"You didn't," Brennan reminded him. "So how do you feel about being one now?"

"I guess it's possible to change your mind, right?" Cash asked him. Brennan had vowed to stay single, probably partly because of seeing how hard Cash's divorce had been on him.

Hell, he'd never really recovered from it. He'd never gotten over losing Valentina.

"Is it?" Patrick asked the question now, arching one of his light brown eyebrows over one of his hazel eyes. He sat on the edge of the bed across from Cash.

"It's really hard for us Coltons," Brennan said. "But it is possible."

Ashlynn snorted. "Not for all of us Coltons. I'm over dating. So over it…" Her forehead creased beneath the lock of dark hair that had escaped from her ponytail and fallen across it.

"You didn't call this meeting for us all to discuss our personal lives," Cash reminded them, embarrassed that his had taken over the conversation. He was also embarrassed over how badly he'd screwed up his personal life.

If only he could have figured out a way to balance work and his wife…to give them both his attention…

Maybe he wouldn't have lost her. But that had only been part of their problem. The other had been his refusal to start a family with her. Hell, they'd just wanted different things out of life.

"No, I called this meeting to talk about the Landmark Killer without the risk of him overhearing us," Brennan said. "We've been going through these lists of employees from our office and from the 130th Precinct. Using Sinead's profile of a male in his twenties, we've narrowed it down to six. Two rookie cops at the 130th as well as a PI who works out of the precinct a lot."

"And the other three?" Cash asked.

"Are the reason I booked this room for the meeting. They work out of our office," Brennan said.

They'd already suspected that someone close to them was the killer, someone who knew about their personal lives. "Yeah, but who?" Cash asked.

"A researcher, an IT employee and—" he lowered his voice as if he was worried the guy might be lurking outside the hotel room door "—the director's assistant, Xander Washer."

Cash whistled between his teeth. "Good thing the director's out of town. She's not going to appreciate her right hand being a suspect."

Patrick grunted. "Sucks when you can't trust the people you work with…"

They all nodded in agreement. "But it has to be someone close to us," Cash repeated what they'd already suspected. "Someone who knew about our dad and Valentina…"

"Or it could just be someone who did his research on us. Why don't you take Perkins, the researcher?" Brennan asked Cash.

"Jonathan Perkins?" Ashlynn asked.

Brennan nodded. "Yeah."

"He asked me out a few months ago," she admitted. "But I shot him down." She groaned. "So over dating…"

"Probably a good thing you shot him down," Cash said. "He might be a crazed psychopath."

Ashlynn snorted. "Sure, under his sweater vests."

"Maybe your rejection set him off," Brennan

teased. Their family often handled difficult situations by using humor to diffuse them.

"I'll check his alibis for the murders," Cash said.

Brennan divvied up the rest of the suspects, giving Xander Washer to Ashlynn. There was also an IT employee at the FBI, two rookie cops at the 130th and a PI who worked out of there a lot as well. Then he tossed computers at each of them, and they proceeded to deep-dive into the suspects' phone records and credit card invoices, checking specifically the dates and times of the murders.

But Cash was distracted, thinking of Valentina and the kids. His family...

He was worried about them, worried about their safety and worried that the little girls weren't the only ones getting used to him being part of their lives. He was getting used to them as well, to being Daddy to Valentina's Mommy, to being the family he'd sworn he never wanted.

Panic pressed on his chest at the thought, making it hard for him to breathe. So hard that he could only take short, shallow breaths like he was hyperventilating.

"Are you okay?" Patrick asked.

He nodded. "Yeah, yeah, just..."

"Distracted," Brennan finished for him. "You don't have to worry about Valentina and your daughters. Sergeant Percell is at the door. He's protecting the—"

Cash's cell ringing interrupted his twin's assurances. And when Cash saw that it was Dave calling him, he was worried that his brother was wrong. That Dave hadn't protected them at all, and Cash shouldn't have left them.

Luci's fever was not dropping. And she was more listless and dehydrated. She needed to get to the doctor's office fast. Even though she didn't use it often, Valentina had a car parked in the garage beneath the condo building; she could drive the twins herself. She shouldn't have waited for Cash to come back. She should have just shoved his friend aside and carried her kids out.

But when Sergeant Percell had handed his cell phone to her, Cash had been on it, vowing that he was close and that he would be there right away.

Even if he was on his way and it wouldn't take him long, those precious moments with a sick child felt interminably long to Valentina as she paced the living room as she waited for him.

The medicine and Pedialyte hadn't worked. Even a cool bath hadn't lowered Luci's fever. The poor kid was so sick that Valentina's heart ached for her. Luci was always so energetic and upbeat and usually very healthy. She didn't get sick, not like this. Sniffles had been the most serious illness the little girl had ever had.

Valentina was scared, especially after how she'd lost her grandparents. She couldn't lose a child, too. When the knock finally came at the door, she was ready, the children already in their double stroller. She jerked open the door.

"You're supposed to wait to confirm who is knocking," Cash admonished her.

And her fury bubbled over. "I've been waiting long enough. No, Luci has. She needs medical attention right away."

Cash bent over the stroller. While Ana was awake, she was quiet as if she felt Valentina's fear. Or maybe she was so attuned to her twin that she knew how sick she was, that this was serious. Luci slept, slumped in her seat in the stroller. "She's so flushed," Cash remarked, his deep voice gruff with emotion. "Let's get her to the ER."

"My doctor's office is in the urgent care center not far from here," she said. "They're like a small emergency room and are ready to set up an IV to treat her."

"I'm sorry," Cash said as he stepped back and helped her get the stroller through the doorway. Then he guided it down the hall toward the elevator that Sergeant Percell was holding open for them. "I didn't know. I wouldn't have left if I knew she was sick."

Valentina felt a twinge of regret for being short with him. She hadn't known, either; she should have checked on the twins sooner, should have found out why the kids had been so tired as to fall asleep in the morning. She wanted to comfort Cash, but she needed comfort, too.

No. She needed to focus on her children; she'd let Cash and her desire for him distract her from that, from what mattered most.

She pushed the stroller into the elevator and barely

waited for Sergeant Percell and Cash to step inside before she closed the doors and pressed the button for the basement. Once the elevator started its descent, she crouched down in front of the stroller. "You'll be feeling better soon," she assured Luci.

But the child didn't open her eyes, as if the lids were too heavy to lift; they just fluttered a bit. A quiet murmur slipped through her lips though as if she was trying to tell Valentina something.

"She said Daddy," Ana translated for her.

And Cash sucked in a breath before he crouched down in front of the stroller next to Valentina. "You're going to be okay, sweetheart," he told the little girl, and he brushed his fingers across her flushed cheek.

Luci's lips curved slightly as if she'd heard him and believed him.

Valentina wished she had the same faith. But the little girl's fever hadn't come down; her body was working too hard trying to fight whatever virus she'd picked up. Probably at day care...

Though it had taken a week for it to get her this sick, Valentina should have seen the earlier signs. Luci was the one who loved going to the amusement park, who loved being outside, but she hadn't pushed once to leave the condo.

Valentina had thought it was because of the novelty of Cash staying with them that the girls had been happy to stay inside with their new daddy. But now she wondered...

She reached out and checked Ana's forehead, too,

but it was still cool, like it had been. She wasn't sick yet, but she usually got what Luci had. Actually, she usually had it first and the worst.

"Let me know if you start feeling bad, too," she told her.

"I 'kay, Mommy," she replied. "Luci sick."

"Yes, but we're getting her to the doctor now." And Valentina would have the pediatrician check out Ana, too.

The elevator dinged as it finally stopped in the garage. The trip had seemed to take forever, just as it had for Cash to get here. Tears of frustration stung Valentina's eyes. She just wanted to scoop them up and run with them to the doctor, to get them help.

But Cash held the stroller back and her as the sergeant started out first. Dave walked a short distance away from the elevator, turned around and nodded, probably indicating it was all clear.

At least that was what Cash seemed to think because he started out with the stroller. But he pushed it with one hand while he reached for his holster with the other, as if he wasn't entirely sure that there was no danger lurking in the dark shadows of the garage.

Valentina was more worried about Luci's fever. That was the real threat to her child. Not some car careening out of nowhere at them again like had happened a week ago.

She shouldn't have let Cash hold them hostage in the condo the last week like he pretty much had. She should have made sure that the girls got out, got fresh air, and maybe Luci wouldn't have gotten so sick.

Tears of frustration stung her eyes, and she wanted to hurl accusations at him, to blame this illness on him. But before she could open her mouth, someone stepped from the shadows. Wearing dark clothes with a hoodie pulled tight around his face, he looked like a shadow but for the glint of his eyes in the darkness and the glint of the gun he held.

Ana screamed. "Bad man!"

And Cash drew his weapon just as the man pointed his gun toward them.

She wasn't sure who fired first, just that the gunshots echoed throughout the parking garage. Ana covered her ears and closed her eyes as she screamed. And Valentina's scream echoed her daughter's. She stepped between them, crouching over them, trying to protect them as the elevator doors closed behind them, cutting off their chance of escape.

Cash was between them and the shooter. And she heard his grunt of pain and felt his body jerking as he took a bullet. And she screamed again.

Chapter 13

Cash got hit. But the bullet just grazed his arm, burning more than it hurt. He was worried that after grazing him, the bullet had hit the stroller, though, or Valentina. He had to get them to safety. The elevator doors had closed.

"Dave!" he called out, worried for his friend.

Dave waved to him from behind a pillar he used as a shield. But the shooter wasn't firing in the sergeant's direction. He'd fired at Cash or at Cash's family.

Cash had returned fire, but he wasn't sure if he'd hit the guy, or if he was just hiding. He moved quickly, glad that he'd parked near the elevator. He clicked the locks and got the kids and Valentina into the FBI SUV with its bulletproof glass. They would be safe.

Which was proved when bullets pinged off the vehicle, striking the metal and the windows. He turned toward the direction of the shots, ready to go hunt down the man. But Valentina, who was in the back, yelled, "No. We have to get out of here!"

She was right. For Luci's sake, he needed to get them to the urgent care.

He shut the driver's door and started the ignition, but as he did, the shooter continued to fire at them from somewhere in the shadows. Pressing hard on the accelerator, he sped away, careening around the corners toward the exit to the street. He could only hope that Dave would be okay and that the sergeant would get some shots off that did hit the man. At the moment, protecting his family was Cash's main responsibility, but he called 9-1-1 as well, identified himself and requested backup for Dave. A unit was close, the sirens blaring loudly as he exited the garage.

"You're bleeding," Valentina whispered, her voice raspy from her screaming or from her fear.

That fear gripped him that she was talking to one of the kids. But she reached between the seats, from where she sat in the back with the girls, and touched his arm.

"I'm fine," he insisted, even though the wound was still stinging and burning like the guy had shot a bee through his arm instead of a bullet. His arm was bleeding, though, he could feel the blood trickling over his skin.

"Daddy…" Ana whispered, her voice cracking

with the tears that slid down her face. "The bad man got you, too."

"Too?" he asked, and he chanced another glance into the back seat. "Are you hurt? Is anyone hurt?"

"Sparky…" Ana murmured.

"She must be getting a fever, too," Valentina said as she pushed back the girl's damp curls and touched her forehead.

Cash swallowed a curse. They had enough going on right now with being sick, and he'd brought that damn shooter into their lives. He must have followed Cash from the hotel, somehow gotten into the garage…

Unless he'd been here. Unless he lived here, too.

"What do you know about Blake Highland?" he asked Valentina.

She sucked in a breath. "Why are you asking? He just lives down the hall and drinks too much. That's all I know."

Fortunately the urgent care was close, and he got the girls and Valentina safely inside. As they checked in, he was able to follow up on what had happened in Valentina's garage. Dave was okay. He'd lost the shooter, but he hadn't been hit. Unfortunately, ducking bullets hadn't given him a chance to get a description of the man or the vehicle he'd been driving, if he'd been driving one at all.

One minute he was there, and the next he was gone, the second Cash had driven off. Cash and his family had definitely been the intended target.

"Find out where that Highland guy was. Check

his alibi," Cash advised. Just as he and his unit had alibis they needed to check. He called Brennan next, bringing him up to date on what had just happened.

Brennan cursed. "We're on our way."

Because the hotel was close, it didn't take long before his family stormed into the urgent care waiting room. He could hear their voices from where he was in the back, sitting next to the bed where his little girl was hooked to an IV.

He got up from his chair to head off his family. But Valentina grabbed his uninjured arm and insisted, as she had been insisting since they'd arrived, "You need stitches."

He shrugged off her concern, but he couldn't shrug off his guilt. Somehow this was his fault; he just knew it. Maybe not Luci getting sick, but the shooting and the nearly getting run down had to be. He'd put his family in extreme danger because of his job, because of what he did, hunting serial killers.

That probably meant that the rest of his family was in danger, too. He stepped through the door to the waiting room, and they turned toward him.

"Are you all right?" Ashlynn asked as she rushed toward him. She reached out as if she intended to hug him but jerked back before she touched his arm. "You're bleeding!"

"So I've been told."

"You got shot," Patrick said, his face getting pale.

The co-head of FBI CSI was definitely not squeamish. He was just concerned. They'd already lost their dad; they didn't want to lose anyone else in their family.

"I'm fine," he assured them all. "Just got grazed a little." But with the way blood trickled yet from the wound, Valentina was probably right that he needed stitches. And maybe a tetanus shot. He didn't remember the last time he'd had one.

"What about Valentina and the kids?" Brennan asked, and his face was pale, too, with concern. "How are they doing?"

Cash's heart swelled with gratitude that his siblings cared about his family even though they had yet to meet the girls. "They didn't get hit with bullets—"

"What about the one with the fever?" Patrick interjected to ask.

After he took that call from Dave, he'd explained to them he'd had to leave because his daughter was sick and Valentina was worried. He'd been scared, too, and then the shooting...

"Is she all right?" Brennan asked.

"Luci. She has the flu and is dehydrated. They gave her some medicine and have an IV in her now," Cash said. "And the doctor thinks that once her fever breaks, she'll be fine."

"Can we see them?" Ashlynn asked tentatively.

"I'll check with Valentina," he said. "And the doctor. While Luci's fever is starting to come down, they want to keep monitoring her and Ana to make sure that she isn't getting one. They're both really shaken up over what happened. And scared." His voice cracked as emotion overwhelmed him. "They shouldn't have been scared like that, from the shooting and from the thing with the car. They shouldn't be in danger like that..."

Because of him. He couldn't help but think this was all his fault. And Valentina undoubtedly blamed him, too. But his family, his siblings at least, all gathered around to comfort and embrace him and to make damn sure he got his bullet wound treated.

He was lucky that he had them, like he was lucky that he had the girls in his life now. But he couldn't help but worry that his luck wasn't going to last and that he would lose someone close to him again like they'd lost their dad.

He kept insisting that he was fine, but Valentina had her doubts about him. Maybe he believed what he was saying or he was lying so that he didn't worry the girls, but either way he needed to be treated. He could have been in shock since the shooting.

She was. She'd known that car nearly running them down hadn't been an accident, not when the driver had turned around and tried again. But she hadn't thought that the person might know where she lived, might have gotten access to the parking garage and might have tried to kill them all just steps from their home.

Where she'd always felt so safe and protected and loved and happy with her grandparents and with her children. She'd been resenting Cash for keeping them inside this past week, but clearly his overprotectiveness had been the only thing keeping them safe.

She hadn't.

So when Cash asked if his siblings could come back and meet the girls, she didn't have the heart to say no. The girls were doing better now, health-wise, but they were still afraid and uneasy.

Thinking that maybe meeting their aunt and uncles would distract them, she had agreed to let them come back to meet the girls. When she saw how Brennan and Ashlynn and Patrick immediately fell for the little ones, her tension eased even as her guilt increased. She shouldn't have kept the girls from their family, from their Colton family of dad, uncles, aunt and all the many, many cousins that Cash had.

In comparison Valentina's family was small, especially since her grandparents had died. And her parents spent all their time traveling now, as if they were afraid to stop moving, afraid that if they did, they might stop living. It wasn't retirement that had killed her grandparents, though. It had been an illness.

Fortunately that wasn't the one that Luci had. She was going to be fine. The fever was gone and she was getting rehydrated. She was less sleepy, too, so she answered her uncles' and aunt's questions for both her and Ana, who was too shy to reply for herself.

Or maybe still too scared.

She'd been the one who'd seen the bad man first. Who'd seen the gun…

Valentina had seen him, too, with that cold gleam in his eyes. He had definitely intended to kill them. All of them? But why?

She could think of no reason but for Cash and the killers he hunted. He and his family. Maybe being with all of them put the girls in more danger.

But if Cash hadn't been there…then she and the girls wouldn't be here. They would have died for certain, if not from the car trying to run them down, then they would have died in the parking garage.

Once again Cash had saved their lives. And Valentina had yet to thank him. She felt guilty over that, too, and over how she'd treated him when he'd first shown up at the condo. All he'd wanted was to protect them.

So much so that he'd literally taken a bullet for them. He was lucky he hadn't died. No. She was lucky. She and the girls were lucky to have him as their protector.

But was that self-appointed position going to wind up costing him his life?

The son of a bitch had hit him. Not the cop but the other guy. The one who'd stood in his way, who'd stopped him from eliminating the threat to his freedom.

The bullet had grazed his cheek even through the thick mask, knocking it slightly askew so he hadn't been able to see clearly through the damn eyeholes. If he had been, he wouldn't have missed. At least he'd hit the guy.

He'd been bleeding, too, blood running down his arm and dripping from his hand. The blood left in the garage had to be all his.

He couldn't have left blood, couldn't have left any DNA that could get traced back to him. He was always so damn careful, until that day just before he'd tried running them down. Then he'd gotten sloppy, overconfident and everything had gone so damn wrong.

That wasn't like him; he was usually so careful. He always plotted everything out in advance, and he always made sure that he had insurance, too. A backup plan when things fell apart. A way to protect himself.

But now he'd gotten shot.

He pulled off the heavy ski mask he'd been wearing. It was heavy, saturated with his blood. But it must have caught most of it. And what had escaped from it had trickled down his neck and saturated his shirt. He hadn't left anything behind in that parking garage but the empty shells from his gun. A gun that could be traced to other crimes but not back to him.

He never registered a weapon. Never took any risks that could expose his identity or his culpability. Except that day...

He'd made a mistake then, and there was only one way to fix it: make sure that whole damn family died.

Chapter 14

Cash would have felt uneasy driving back into the parking garage if it wasn't swarming with techs and officers. Some of the techs were from the FBI CSI. One of them being Patrick, who'd insisted on personally checking for evidence, no doubt hoping that he would find something to lead them to the man who'd shot Cash and who'd probably intended to shoot them all.

Fortunately the exhausted girls had fallen asleep in the back of the SUV, or they might have been afraid to return to the parking garage, like Valentina clearly was, her hands knotting in her lap as she sat next to Cash in the passenger seat.

"It's safe now," he assured her in a low whisper.

She nodded. "I know." But her long lashes fluttered as if she was blinking back tears, probably over the close call they'd had, over her babies being in the danger they'd been in because of him.

"I'm sorry," he said as the guilt weighed so heavily on him that his shoulders bowed with it.

She glanced across the console at him. "Why? For what? You saved our lives again."

"I can't help but think I'm the reason your lives have needed saving," he said.

Brennan was considering it even more of a possibility now that this was related to them and not Valentina. Even if it wasn't the Landmark Killer, it might be someone else they'd put away, or a fan of someone else they'd brought to justice.

Like the Landmark Killer was an obsessed fan of the Black Widow, Maeve O'Leary.

"You were right," she said.

He flinched.

"There is a lot of evil in the world," she said.

She had always been so bright and optimistic, so happy. He hated that the darkness of his world was casting a shadow over hers. And over the little girls.

A soft sigh emanated from the back seat and a little snore. She looked back at their daughters and smiled, love radiating from her. She was the good that was necessary in the world to balance out the bad.

She was too good for Cash. He'd figured that out too late, though.

"They need to get up to their beds," she said. And she opened her door, stepped out and opened the back door. She had Ana in her arms already when he picked up Luci. "Your arm!" she gasped with concern. "You're hurt. You shouldn't be trying to carry her."

"It's still numb," he lied. "From when they stitched it up." The local anesthesia had actually worn off before they'd left the urgent care, leaving his arm throbbing with a dull ache. But that pain was nothing compared to the ache in his heart when he thought of how close he'd come to losing them.

Even though he'd only had them in his life for a week, he couldn't imagine it without them now. Without her…

But he hadn't just had to imagine that; he'd lived that reality for the past three years when he'd lived without Valentina.

He held Luci close as they headed toward the elevator. Dave was there, holding open the doors for them. Valentina stepped inside first, and as Cash followed her, he told his old friend, "I'm glad you're okay."

Dave shook his head. "I wish I'd gotten him, but he was there and gone…like a ghost."

Luci tensed in his arms as if she'd heard them, as if their talk had scared her. "Shh…" Cash murmured to her. "It's okay. You're safe."

Dave shushed as well and stepped back so that the elevator doors could close. Valentina pushed the button for her floor, then leaned back against the wall as if exhausted.

She probably was. The girls woke up early every day and then this day…

So much had happened.

So much worse could have happened.

When the doors opened, Cash peered out first. There was an officer at the door to her apartment. Dave must have sent him up first to make sure the hallway was secure for their arrival. Could the shooter have gone inside the building?

Could he still be here?

"The area is secure, Agent Colton," the young officer said as if she'd read Cash's mind. "We didn't have a key to the door, but the lock hasn't been tampered with. Unless they had a key to get inside, the unit should still be secure, too."

"Nobody else has a key," Valentina said as she fumbled hers from her bag and, juggling the child sleeping against her, managed to unlock the door.

Another door creaked open down the hall, and Cash caught sight of Blake Highland peering out of his unit. Highland had the code to the parking garage, the code Valentina had had to share with Cash for him to get in and out. "Hurry up," Cash said as Valentina pushed open her door.

When his gaze collided with Cash's, Blake shut the door again. But Cash was still on edge until Valentina stepped inside her condo. Even after he followed her in and she dead-bolted the door again, he wasn't totally at ease.

"Let's put them down in their beds," she whispered at him with a worried glance at his shoulder.

The stitches were starting to strain, but if the wound was bleeding again, it wouldn't be possible to tell as bloody as the sleeve of his shirt already was. He didn't want to get any of that on Luci, though. He just wanted to tuck her back into her little bed where she'd be safe and hopefully dream sweet dreams despite the scary incident in the parking garage.

That had been too damn close a call for all of them. Why would anyone want to hurt Valentina and the two little girls, though? It didn't make sense. But then evil seldom made sense to anyone but the evildoer.

Like the Landmark Killer.

Who really thought his killing in Maeve O'Leary's name was going to gain her release…

Especially if he worked in law enforcement at the 130th Precinct or at the FBI, he had to know better, had to know that wasn't how justice worked.

If justice worked…

Sometimes killers managed to escape it, to either never get caught or never serve time behind bars. That couldn't happen this time.

Valentina settled Ana into her bed and tucked her under her covers. Then she pulled back the blankets on Luci's bed. He hugged the little girl close for a moment before he settled her onto her pink sheets. Then Valentina pulled up the blankets again and kissed the little girl's forehead. She released a soft sigh that stirred Luci's curls.

"She's still cool," she said. "The fever hasn't come back. She's recovering from being sick."

But would they recover from the attempts on their lives? Valentina must have been worried because she stared at them both for a long moment, her brow furrowed with her concern, before she backed out of the room into the hall.

Cash followed her out and once again he whispered, "I'm sorry."

"You're not responsible for the evil," Valentina said. "It's not your fault that it exists."

"It's my job to stop it," he said.

"A job you work harder at than most people work in their lives," she said. "There's only so much you can do. You can't take responsibility for everything bad that happens."

"I take responsibility for us," he said. "For our divorce…"

Her lips curved into a slight smile. "Since you're the one who filed, you should."

"But you were the one who left," he said. "Because I couldn't give you what you wanted, the family…"

Her smile widened a bit and she glanced over her shoulder into the girls' room. "But you did…" Then she turned back to him and her smile slipped away. "And I'm sorry I didn't tell you about them. That I didn't share them with you and with your family."

"Their aunt and uncles are going to spoil them," he said, remembering how the little girls had charmed his siblings. Brennan, Patrick and Ashlynn had fallen for them nearly as quickly and hard as he had.

As he'd fallen for Valentina all those years ago…

And he felt himself tumbling now, so much so that he swayed on his feet and reached out to grasp the wall.

"Cash," she said with alarm, and she reached for him, sliding her arms around him. "You need to go to bed, too. You're injured and you've lost blood." But instead of guiding him toward the living room and the couch, she turned him toward her room.

"Valentina?" he asked when she guided him through the doorway toward her bed.

"You're injured. You can't sleep on the couch tonight," she said. "You can have my bed."

He shook his head. "I can't take it."

"You have to," she insisted. "You need your rest. You're barely able to stand right now you're so exhausted."

While her concern touched him, his male pride bristled and he pulled away from her. "I'm fine. Really. It was just…"

"What?" she asked.

"You," he admitted, "you still get to me, Valentina."

Her dark eyes widened with surprise. Then she sighed and said, "You still get to me, too, Cash."

A stunned silence followed her admission. Cash didn't say anything for a long moment; then his throat moved as if he was struggling to swallow. Concern for him shot through her again. "Cash, you are not okay. Do you need painkillers? Sleep? A shower?"

He seemed to struggle to speak, his mouth open for a few moments before words rasped out of him. "I need you."

"Damn it," she murmured.

"What?" he asked, his body tense.

"I need you, too."

She didn't want to, but it was undeniable. And after how close she'd come to losing him in that parking garage, she couldn't waste another minute like she'd wasted the entire week fighting her desire for him.

He didn't move, stood frozen in place as if her admission had shocked him. She had kind of shocked herself with making it. But now that she'd admitted it, she couldn't take it back or take back the desire she felt for him.

So she stepped forward and reached for him again like she had in the hall. When she slid her arms around his waist, she turned and guided him toward the bathroom. "You need to clean up," she said as she closed the door and locked it behind them, just in case the girls woke up.

He grimaced. "The blood. I don't want to get any of it on you."

"And the bandage needs to stay dry," she reminded him. Once inside the bathroom, instead of starting the shower, she turned on the faucet and filled the tub.

"Join me," Cash implored her, his green eyes dark with desire, his pupils entirely dilated.

Despite his injured arm, he had no problem undressing. Once again he stashed his weapon where there was no way the girls could reach it on the top shelf of the linen closet. He loved them as much as she did and wanted to keep them safe, so much so that he'd stepped in front of a bullet for them.

It was no wonder she was falling for him all over again, even though she knew it wouldn't work out any differently than it had last time. She would always want more of him than he had left from his crusade against evil to give her. But now she wasn't going to worry about the future; she was only going to focus on the present.

And Cash…

Once he'd stripped off his clothes, leaving him bare but for that bandage on his arm, he reached for her.

But Valentina stepped back and pulled her dress over her head. Then she unclipped her bra and let it drop away before sliding down her panties.

He gasped as if he was in physical pain again. And maybe with the way his body was reacting, he was.

She was, her breasts aching for his touch. Her core throbbing, begging for release.

He stepped closer, but his arms stayed at his sides. He didn't touch her. "Are you sure?" he asked, his voice raw with the desire that burned in his green-eyed gaze.

"Yes," she assured him.

But still he didn't reach for her. So she was the one who wrapped her arms around his neck and pulled his head down for her kiss. And it was as if her kiss gave him the permission he'd been waiting for, and he kissed her back passionately, his mouth making love to hers.

And finally he touched her, sliding his hands all over her body, caressing every inch of skin before he cupped her breasts and stroked his thumbs across her nipples.

She moaned in his mouth. And he moved one hand lower, between her legs, lightly touching her, stroking her. She parted her legs a little bit, and he slid a finger inside her.

And he groaned. Pulling back, he panted for breath and murmured, "You're so hot. So wet…"

So ready for him.

He lifted her up then, settling her onto the counter between the double vanities. And instead of joining their bodies, he dropped to his knees. "I have to taste you…"

His breath was hot between her legs, his tongue stroking over her clit before sliding inside her. And he made love to her with his mouth.

She arched her neck, and his hands cupped her breasts, teasing the nipples again. Pleasure shot through her, the pressure finally breaking in a climax that had her shuddering with release. She bit her lip to hold back the cry. And even though the orgasm left her limp with pleasure, it wasn't enough. She wanted him.

So she tugged on his shoulders, pulling him up from the floor. And she slid her hand over his pulsating cock, down the length of it. He groaned and gritted his teeth, and muscles twitched along his jaw and one at the side of his neck.

"The water's going to get cold," she warned him, even as she tugged on his erection.

"Condom," he gritted.

She shook her head. "I had to regulate my periods, so I got another IUD. A better one. It's safe. You won't accidentally get me pregnant again."

He shook his head now. "They weren't an accident. They were a blessing."

And she fell even harder for him, tears stinging her eyes that he'd said that, that he clearly felt that way about his daughters. She'd been so worried.

He touched her cheek then. "Did you think I would be mad? Is that why you didn't tell me?"

"I didn't want you to think I was trying to trap you or get you back…"

"I wouldn't have thought that," he assured her.

She didn't want to talk anymore about the past. She'd made too many mistakes, cost him three years with his daughters that she couldn't give back to him. But she could give him the release he'd given her.

When she leaned over, though, to close her lips around his erection, he caught her shoulders and held her up. "I need to be inside you," he said. "I need to feel you…"

And then he was there, his erection filling her. He thrust in and out, and she wrapped her legs around him, holding him tight, matching his rhythm as the pressure built inside her again.

Despite the orgasm he'd already given her, she was frantic and desperate for release. She clutched at him, pulling him deep, using her inner muscles to squeeze him.

He gritted his teeth and groaned, sweat beading

on his forehead. Then he reached between their bodies and stroked her, and she came apart in his arms.

His body shuddered as he joined her. But even after, he trembled a little. Probably with exhaustion and with pain from his injury. Blood seeped through that bandage, staining it.

And a pang of guilt struck her. "You need that bath," she said. "And rest."

"I needed you."

She'd needed him, too, not just now but the last three years. Honestly, she'd needed him before that, throughout the three years of their marriage, but she'd never quite had him. At least not enough of him…

His job had always been more important than their marriage. She didn't expect that to change now even with the girls in his life. In fact, having daughters to protect would probably make him even more determined to rid the world of evil…

She'd felt selfish for wanting more of him then. But now she wasn't thinking just of herself. She was thinking of Luci and Ana, too.

They deserved more.

So did she.

Chapter 15

Cash would have suspected he'd dreamed the night before, the lovemaking with Valentina, if not for waking up in her bed where they'd made love again after the bathroom.

He wished he'd dreamed the rest of what had happened, of the masked man firing at them in the parking garage. But the bandage on his throbbing upper arm verified that it had really happened; it hadn't been just a nightmare.

And that bullet had come too damn close to them. He could hear the girls elsewhere in the condo, talking and giggling. They weren't sick and sleepy today. And they didn't sound scared, either.

That had been his biggest fear, that these attempts on their lives would change them. Would take away their innocence and trust like that serial killer had his when he'd taken his dad's life. Cash had to make sure nobody took *them* away from him. That they were safe…

Instead of leaving the bedroom, he stayed in it, making calls, checking his computer. Working. He had to focus on the case now, for everyone's sake.

The only blood Patrick had found in the garage was the blood Cash had shed. So neither he nor Dave had hit that son of a bitch. Was the man just that good? That much of a professional that Ashlynn suspected he was? Or was he just lucky?

He touched base with Dave, who'd interviewed other condo owners in the building. Everybody claimed that they hadn't been in the parking garage when the shots had been fired. They hadn't seen anything.

When Cash snorted, Dave reminded him, "We didn't see anything either, and we were there."

"Dark clothes, some kind of knit face mask this time…" Not the Mardi Gras one that the first theater victim, the one who'd survived, had said that the Landmark Killer had been wearing when he'd shot him.

What if this wasn't the Landmark Killer? Then they would have two killers to find.

"Did you check out that Blake Highland?" he asked.

"A couple DUIs," Dave said. Then he hesitated a moment before adding, "And a stalking charge…"

Cash cursed.

"Stalking charge was him following around an ex-girlfriend," Dave clarified. "Showing up at her work, at bars where she went and outside her apartment. There was no mention of firearms, and he doesn't have any registered to him."

"That doesn't mean he doesn't have them," Cash said.

"Yeah, but we don't have enough on him to get a search warrant for his place. Plus, I don't think a sloppy drunk would have been able to get the jump on us in that garage and then escape like he did."

"I would hope not," Cash said. But he'd been distracted ever since that text had come about his *sad ex-wife*.

She didn't sound sad now as her laughter drifted, like music, in from the living room. Then the little girls' giggles followed.

And such warmth flooded Cash's chest that he had to put his hand over it, had to feel if it was as warm on the outside as it was inside. Maybe he was getting Luci's fever.

Or maybe it was just love...

"This guy really does seem like a pro," Dave continued, "or maybe somebody in law enforcement."

Like the Landmark Killer. Cash couldn't share that suspicion with Dave, though. The fewer people who knew about their suspects the better. The Landmark Killer was already too close to the case and much too close to them.

Had that been him in the garage last night? Or someone else?

"Thanks for checking into Highland," Cash said. "I'm working on some angles myself. I'll let you know what I find out." After disconnecting that call, he turned his attention to his laptop and Jonathan Perkins's credit card invoices. The next calls he made were to the establishments where there were charges on the dates, around the times of the murders. The ones that retained customers' signatures on receipts agreed to scan and send them over to him. He had a feeling that the suspect he'd been assigned was not the killer.

That left five other suspects out there, and one of them was determined to kill again until all the letters of Maeve O'Leary's name were spelled out with the first letter of the victims' names. Eleven victims.

Eleven lives that would be lost if they couldn't catch and stop this guy. And what about other lives he might take as collateral damage?

Like Valentina and Ana and Luci…

He didn't want them to be collateral damage in this crusade of his and his unit to stop the serial killer. He didn't want to lose them to anyone, but most especially not to an evil that he'd brought into their lives.

Valentina knew Cash was awake because she could hear the deep rumble of his voice coming from the bedroom. He was on the phone, as he had so often been during their marriage. Even when he hadn't been in the office, he had never been completely with her…unless they'd been making love.

She drew in a shaky breath and forced her mind from that, from what had happened between them. From how incredibly good it had felt…

And she thought of his work instead. She understood how important his job was, and she would never want to stop him from doing it. She'd just gotten tired of it consuming him 24/7. Of his professional life leaving no room for a personal life.

For her.

She'd had a professional life, too. She loved being a librarian, connecting people with the books they needed for enjoyment or research or escape. She missed her job, missed interacting with all the library patrons.

She wasn't the only one missing her life outside this condo. The girls had been mentioning their day care friends this morning as well. They missed going to "school" as they called it. They needed to get their lives back. Their routine…

But she also remembered how she'd felt the day before with all the shooting in the parking garage. And she knew it wasn't safe for them to leave. Not yet.

Not until this person was caught, and she and the girls were no longer in danger.

Cash probably always would be, because he hunted down serial killers like they hunted their victims. Those brutal killers didn't want to be caught, to be stopped, so they would always turn on the ones trying to track them down.

Would they always come after the investigators'

families, too? Would she and the girls always be in danger because of him? Maybe she should have never admitted that the girls were his. But there was no mistaking that they were with how much they acted and looked like him.

She needed to take her mind off the danger, and off what had happened the night before, of her making love with him. That might have been the most danger she'd been in, the danger of falling for him all over again, of thinking that they could make it work this time, of getting used to sleeping with him, curled up in his arms, her head on his chest, as she had every night they'd been married.

Or at least the nights he'd actually come home...

He'd pulled so many all-nighters at the office as well as doing overnight travel, tracking serial killers across the country. She'd been on her own a lot, so she hadn't thought moving out would feel that different than living with him. But it had. She'd missed him. And she'd grown to appreciate that even if they'd had just a little bit of time together, it had been better than nothing.

But then the divorce papers had arrived from his lawyer.

And she'd realized that even if she was willing to compromise to make their marriage work, he hadn't been willing or even interested. So she'd focused then on building her own life on Coney Island in the condo she'd inherited and loved. And when she'd finally realized that she had more than just a long case of the flu, she'd expanded that life to include the family she'd always wanted.

Her daughters.

She'd been so scared for their future yesterday. First with Luci and the fever that wouldn't go down, and then during the shooting…

But Cash had protected them, even taking a bullet for them. So it was no wonder she'd given in to her feelings for him, to the desire.

But she couldn't do that again; she had to protect her heart like he'd protected them. She couldn't trust him with it again, not after he'd already broken it once.

She drew in a shaky breath and reached for her cell phone. She'd checked in a couple of times with the library, answering any questions anyone might have had for her as well as making sure that her job would be there for her when it was safe for her return. The last thing she wanted to do was put any of her coworkers or library patrons in danger if someone tried to get to her there like they had on the street and in the parking garage.

She shivered despite the sunlight pouring through the windows, warming the condo. Then she dialed work, wanting to stay connected to the life she'd put on hold.

"Coney Island Library Co-op," a male voice answered the phone.

"Randall," she greeted her coworker. "This is Valentina."

"Valentina, how are you?" he asked. "I saw on the

news that there was a shooting in the parking garage of your building. Are you and the girls all right?"

"Yes, we are," she assured him. Thanks to Cash. "How are you doing? Everything okay at the library?"

"Yes, people missing you like crazy," he said. "Including me."

"That's sweet," she said. "I miss you all, too." And she wanted to get back to her own life before she got used to this life, the one with Cash home every day with her and the girls. She knew it would never be like that in real life. "How is Mrs. Miller?" she asked. "Did she pick up the memoir she wanted to read?"

"I left her a message when it came in on Monday, but she hasn't come by for it yet," he said.

She furrowed her brow, wondering why it would have taken her so long. The older woman didn't live far from the library and usually stopped by every couple of days even if she wasn't waiting for a book to come in.

"That's odd," she said. "Do you have her number? I can give her a call. No. Never mind, I think I have it." The woman had put her contact information into Valentina's phone a while ago with the offer of helping out with the girls if Valentina had ever needed it. She was such a sweet woman.

Valentina should have called her earlier, so that she wouldn't worry about her not being around the library. But then it sounded as if Mrs. Miller hadn't been there either, or for certain she would have picked up the book she'd been anxious to read.

Hoping that everything was okay with Mrs. Miller, she quickly ended her call with Randall, scrolled through her contacts until she found Mrs. Miller's and called. The cell went to an automated message that said the call could not go through at this time. But the woman also had a landline, so Valentina tried that next.

"Hello?" a man answered the phone.

Valentina froze for a moment. She'd thought the older woman was a widow living alone. "I'm sorry. I might have the wrong number. I'm looking for Mrs. Miller."

"So are we," the male voice replied.

"Why? What's happened?" she asked, fear and concern gripping her.

"Who are you?" the male voice asked.

"I'm—"

A big hand covered hers, pulling the cell away from her ear. "What's going on?" Cash asked her. "Who are you talking to?"

She shrugged. "I don't know. I'm trying to get hold of one of my library patrons but someone else answered her phone. I have a bad feeling…" It churned with nerves in her stomach now, making her feel sick. Had something happened to Mrs. Miller? Was that why she hadn't been around the library this past week?

Cash took the cell phone from her and lifted it to his ear. "This is Special Agent Cash Colton," he said. "Who are you?" He frowned, a line appearing between his eyebrows as he listened to the reply. "How long has she been missing?"

Valentina gasped and pressed a hand to her heart. "Mrs. Miller is missing?"

"How do you know her?" Cash asked, and now he held out the phone on speaker. "Detective Bentley, this is Valentina Acosta Colton. My wife."

Ex. But she didn't correct him. That wasn't as important as finding out what had happened to Mrs. Miller.

"I'm a librarian," she told the officer on the phone. "Mrs. Miller comes into the library every couple of days. I was just touching base with my work, and nobody has seen her all week and that is definitely unusual for her." Especially when she was waiting for a specific book.

"When is the last time you saw her?" the detective asked.

"I…" She drew in a shaky breath, remembering what day. "A week ago yesterday. A Friday…" The Friday that the vehicle had nearly run them down. She glanced up at Cash, wondering if he wanted her to mention that, but he shook his head.

Maybe he thought it had nothing to do with Mrs. Miller's disappearance. And hopefully it didn't.

"Surely someone's seen her since then?" she asked the detective.

"We're checking with her neighbors. It was her doorman who reported her missing. He said, like you did, that she was always out and about, going somewhere at least every couple of days. We're just checking now, trying to find family or where she might have gone."

"I don't think she had family. She'd been a widow for quite a while," Valentina said. "I am concerned…" She glanced at the girls, who were sitting on the couch watching cartoons. Hopefully they weren't paying their conversation any attention. "Mrs. Miller always wore a lot of expensive-looking jewelry. Maybe someone mugged her for it."

"Sparky…" Ana murmured.

And Valentina glanced over at her; she must have been referring to something on TV. But that was what they'd said when they'd seen Mrs. Miller the last time that Valentina had in the library and the sunlight had been reflecting off all the stones in her jewelry. Hopefully that hadn't been the last time anyone saw the older woman.

"It does look like someone's been in her apartment," the detective admitted. "Things have been gone through. Hard to know what's been taken, though. Have you been here before, Mrs. Colton?"

"A couple of times," she said. "I dropped off books for her when she wasn't feeling well last year, but I didn't pay much attention to her apartment. I wouldn't know what's missing or not." Except for Mrs. Miller. Why was she missing?

"What has been done to find Mrs. Miller so far?" Cash asked.

"The usual. We checked hospital and morgues," the detective replied. "But there were no unidentified females in her age range."

Valentina breathed a little sigh of relief then. That was good. That meant she was probably alive. Maybe she'd just gone on an impromptu trip somewhere. "She was writing her memoir," Valentina said. "She may have reached out to old friends." She'd wanted to write more about them than doing any kissing and telling of her own, as she'd put it to Valentina the last time they'd talked. "Maybe she has taken a trip somewhere…"

"Did she mention anyone in particular?" the detective asked.

"No, but she did have me find a memoir for her about a former Broadway star. I think they knew each other…" She shared the name of the star with the detective.

"She's been dead for a while," Bentley remarked. "She can't be visiting her."

"No," Valentina agreed. At least she hoped that wasn't the case; she hoped Mrs. Miller was still alive.

The detective and Cash talked for a little bit longer, but Valentina tuned out of the rest of their conversation as she kept thinking of the older woman, of how vibrant and full of life she was. She had to be okay.

She didn't even realize Cash had ended the conversation until he handed her cell back to her, its screen dark with the call ended.

"Sorry for interrupting," he said. "But when I heard what sounded like someone asking you intrusive questions—"

"Who I am is intrusive?" she teased him.

Cash had answered for her, calling her his wife. But she wasn't. Not anymore. And she wasn't sure if she ever could be again even if he asked.

"I'm sorry," he said again.

She wondered if he was referring to interrupting her call or last night. Or…

The divorce.

And with two little girls sneaking glances at them, she couldn't ask. So she focused on what mattered most at the moment. Besides the girls.

"Can you help find Mrs. Miller?" she asked. "I know you have a lot of other stuff going on, but I'm really worried about her."

"I doubt her disappearance has anything to do with what's happened recently." He glanced at the girls as well. "She's probably just gone out of town—"

"Without telling the doorman?" she asked. "She'd want him to hold her mail or packages. And she was waiting for that book, too. And if she was leaving, I really think she would have told me that day that the girls and I saw her." Tears stung her eyes as she worried about the older woman, worried about what might have happened to her. She was so sweet. And so alone.

Cash reached for her, closing his arms around her. "I will try to find her," he said. "I'll have Ashlynn do some digging, see if Mrs. Miller recently used her credit cards or booked airfare."

She released a sigh of relief. "Thank you," she said, and she wanted to hug him back, wanted to lay her head on his chest, but she saw the girls, standing now on the couch, staring at them.

She'd already been worried about their getting too attached to him being here, with them, but now she was worried about confusing them, about them thinking that they were that traditional family of mom and dad and kids all living together, all loving each other.

And she was worried that she was beginning to think that, too.

Eli Smith. *E.* The last letter in *Maeve*. The perfect victim. Blond, blue-eyed and in his midthirties.

And now the Landmark Killer had the perfect location for the murder. Or at least the body drop, where that special team of FBI agents would be certain to find it and understand what it meant. How close he was to them.

Far closer than any of them realized…

Chapter 16

"Ride horsey," Luci said, pointing out the living room window toward the bright lights on the rides at Luna Park. "Ride horsey."

Cash held the little girl in his arms, grateful that she was feeling better. Yesterday had been so scary for so many reasons. Her fever. The shooting.

And then last night and the feelings that kept overwhelming him after making love with Valentina. He wanted to do it again. So badly...

It was already past the girls' bedtime. But Valentina wasn't being as strict about it tonight, as if she was reluctant to be alone with him.

Did she regret what had happened between them?

He couldn't regret it, and he couldn't stop wanting to repeat it. He couldn't stop wanting her. He'd tried the past three years, and he'd failed dismally.

"Horsey," Ana echoed from Valentina's arms. She held up the other little girl to stare out the window while he held up Luci.

"They love Luna Park," Valentina said.

"Do you take them there a lot?" he asked.

She nodded. "Every weekend, but…"

Last weekend. When he'd come to stay with them after the incident with the car.

"Ride horsey?" Luci asked. And she touched his face, as if trying to get his attention.

"Soon," he said.

"School…" Ana murmured, and finally she was getting sleepy, her head dropping onto her mother's shoulder.

"School," Luci repeated.

They wanted their old lives back, their routines. He understood even as he realized he didn't want that for himself anymore. Not his usual routine of working around the clock. But how could he stop when there was a killer on the loose?

Especially if that killer was the one who was threatening and making those attempts on the lives of Valentina and the girls…

The Landmark Killer hadn't claimed another victim in over a week, as if he had been busy with something else.

With trying to kill Valentina and the girls?

It had to be him. Nothing else made sense to Cash.

But then there was that woman missing. Valentina's friend.

Ashlynn had run down Mrs. Miller's credit card invoices and verified there had been no charges since she'd visited a salon on that Friday morning, the day that Valentina had seen her last at the library.

Could it have anything to do with…

Flashing lights on the street below caught his attention, fear gripping him that something had happened in the building again. But the lights continued on toward Luna Park.

"Sparky," Luci said.

Ana shook her head. "Not Sparky…"

"Flashing," Valentina clarified. "Those are flashing lights." She met Cash's gaze, and her dark eyes were full of concern.

He doubted those had anything to do with her friend, but he had a feeling in his gut, a churning of dread, that those lights had something to do with someone else.

His phone buzzed in his pocket. And he swung Luci down in order to take the call. As if Valentina didn't want the girls overhearing his conversation, she took Luci's hand and led her out of the room as she carried Ana toward their bedroom.

He probably didn't want them overhearing his conversation, either. "Hey," he answered Brennan's call.

"Sounds like another body might have just turned up," he said.

"Let me guess where…" Cash murmured. "Coney Island."

Brennan groaned with his frustration. "Yup, Luna Park."

"I just saw the lights heading that direction." And he'd instinctively known that something bad had happened. "He's messing with me. First the text about Valentina and then the other things and now this…"

"You don't have to come," Brennan said. "You were hurt last night—"

"I'm fine," he insisted. And the wound wasn't bothering him anymore except that the stitches were starting to itch.

"It might be a trap to get you out of the condo, get you away from Valentina and the girls," Brennan warned him.

"I don't think so," Cash said. "I think this is about Maeve O'Leary and his sick quest to free her."

Brennan groaned again. "Yeah, I'm on my way there. I told the local precinct not to touch anything. And I am sending a couple officers to Valentina's place, to make sure you're all safe."

"Make sure they're safe," Cash agreed. "I'm coming out to the scene, too."

"Patrick's heading up the team to process it," Brennan said. "I told Ashlynn to sit it out just in case it's a trap to bring her out, too."

"I don't think it's Jonathan Perkins," Cash said. "His alibis for the murders all checked out. I got the receipts to back it up."

Brennan released a ragged breath. "That's good. Hopefully it's not one of ours…"

"How else would he know so much about us, though?" Cash asked.

"Daddy! Daddy!" a little voice called out to him from the bedroom, pulling Cash's attention from his call while also pulling at his heart with yearning. He hated having to leave them.

"I don't know," Brennan was saying. "Want me to pick you up? I'm getting close to Valentina's building now."

"Yes, I'll meet you," Cash said.

"Daddy! Daddy!" another voice called out.

"Are you sure?" Brennan asked. Maybe he'd heard the girls calling for Cash.

Calling him Daddy...

He wondered if he would ever get used to it, if his heart would ever stop reacting to the sounds of their voices. He loved them. So much. And because he did, the best thing he could do for them right now was to find whoever was threatening them and stop him for once and for all. Then they could go back to their school during the week and the rides at Luna Park on their weekends.

"I'll be down in just a couple of minutes," he told Brennan. Then he disconnected the call and rushed through the living room to the girls' bedroom.

"Daddy!" Ana exclaimed.

"Daddy, read us the story," Luci said. "Mommy did it. Mommy did it a lot."

"They need new stories," she remarked with a smile that didn't reach her dark eyes. She was upset.

Over all the things the girls were being denied? The park. Their books. Their school.

Or had she overheard his conversation with Brennan?

"I can't read to you right now," Cash said. "Uncle Brennan is coming to pick me up for work."

"It's dark out," Ana said, her little voice cracking with nerves.

"Some people have to work in the dark," he said. And on weekends and holidays and birthdays and anniversaries. He'd missed so much with Valentina even when they'd been married. He understood that was probably why she hadn't told him about the girls; she hadn't wanted him to disappoint them on all those days like he always had disappointed her.

"Why?" Luci asked, her bottom lip sticking out with the stubbornness she'd probably inherited from him.

"Because bad guys don't stop working when it gets dark." In fact, that was when some of them started, so that they could hide in the shadows and elude capture, just like the Landmark Killer had been doing.

"Get the bad guy, Daddy," Ana said as if imploring him. "Get 'im. Bang bang."

Valentina gasped as she stared at her daughter with concern. "Honey, we don't want anyone to get shot…"

"Bang bang," Ana repeated, her dark eyes filling with tears.

"I'll be safe," he promised her. "And you and your sister and Mommy are all very safe here at home."

And he had to do everything he could to keep them safe, to keep the evil away from them.

Even as exhausted as they'd been, Valentina had struggled to get the girls to fall to sleep. Maybe that was because they had been overly tired and emotional. And there'd been so many tears when Cash left.

Some stung her eyes now as she stared out the living room window to where those lights still flashed at Luna Park. That serial killer, the Landmark Killer, had obviously claimed another victim or Cash wouldn't have been called out to the scene.

The girls had been so disappointed that he hadn't stayed to read to them, that he'd had to leave. And after seeing him get shot in the parking garage the day before, they were probably worried about him getting hurt again.

Like she was worried…

Maybe this murder was just to draw him out there, to where those lights flashed at the crime scene. Cash was with his brother and all those other law enforcement personnel, though. He should be safe.

Maybe safer than she and the girls were with him gone. A knock rattled her door, and her pulse quickened. There was supposed to be an officer out there. Cash had assured her of that as he'd left, that she and the girls would be safe even without him.

From the tortured look on his face, it hadn't been all that easy for him to leave the crying twins, either. Or maybe he'd thought that they would be safer without him there, that he was the reason they were in danger.

Valentina wasn't as convinced of that as he was, not since Mrs. Miller had gone missing the same day that car had nearly run them down. The coincidence just seemed too great to her.

The knock came again. And Valentina wasn't sure what to do, who to trust. If it had been Sergeant Percell, she would have felt more secure because she knew him, but it had been another officer out there. And Cash had told her not to open the dead bolt to anyone but him, not even that young female officer.

Valentina had given him the key so that he could unlock it himself when he returned. If he returned…

Even if he was safe at the crime scene, he was all caught up in the case, in catching the killer. She knew how cases like this in the past had consumed him, taking all his time and attention. And this killer was making it even more personal for him and his unit, taunting them with those texts and that article in the *New York Wire.*

"Valentina," a voice called through the door.

A voice she recognized. Ashlynn.

She hurried to the door and turned the dead bolt, pulling it open. "Did something happen? Is Cash all right?" she asked anxiously. He hadn't been gone long, but as the incident in the parking lot had proved, it only took a few seconds for someone to attack and for someone to get hurt.

"As far as I know, he's fine," Ashlynn said. "He

and Brennan and Patrick didn't want me to show up at the scene..."

"Why not?" Valentina asked.

Ashlynn looked away.

And Valentina knew her concerns about Cash's safety were valid. "They're worried it could be a trap."

"And I'm a tech expert, not a special agent like they all are," she said with a sigh of frustration. "I don't carry a gun like they all do."

"I'm glad," Valentina said. "I don't want anything more to do with guns." She shuddered as she remembered what Ana had about Cash getting the bad guy. Bang bang...

Were they becoming so obsessed with guns because of Cash having to use his to protect them first with that car and then again last night?

"I'm actually here to see you," Ashlynn said. "I've been checking into your missing friend."

"Mrs. Miller," Valentina said, her heart fluttering with hope. "Have you found her?"

Ashlynn shook her head. "No, but I wish I had. From what I've been learning about her, she sounds like quite a character. She's known a lot of really interesting people, too."

Valentina nodded. "Yes. I keep telling her to write her memoir, and she said she was starting it."

"Yes, I think she was," Ashlynn said.

"You found notes or her laptop?" Valentina asked.

"So she did have a laptop," Ashlynn mused with a nod.

"Yes."

"That was missing from her apartment. Did she have it with her the day you saw her last?"

"She brought it to the library some days," Valentina said. "But I didn't see it that day. She always carried a big bag with her, though, so it could have been in that."

"I was able to find out who her internet carrier was, and I also tracked down her phone records. She used the same search engine on both," Ashlynn said. "She was looking up people and places and events that had happened in the past…" She shrugged. "Maybe it doesn't mean anything, but she sounds like an interesting woman."

"She is."

"I hope we find her," Ashlynn said.

"Thank you for helping look for her," Valentina said. "I know you have a lot going on with the Landmark Killer…" She glanced out the window toward where those lights flashed not that far away, not nearly far enough away. She and the girls walked there every weekend. Luna Park was closer than the library or day care even. Sometimes they could even hear the shrieks from the Cyclone, of the riders on the famous roller coaster.

She felt a bit like she was on it now with the way her feelings about Cash staying with them were all over the place. High and low.

"I should go," Ashlynn said, but she was peering around the condo. "Are the little ones asleep?"

Valentina nodded and flinched a bit as her head

ached from their crying. The volume and the stress of it. "They were upset when Cash left."

"You're worried they're getting too used to him being around," Ashlynn surmised.

They weren't the only ones she was worried about, but she didn't admit that to Cash's sister.

"I've missed you," Ashlynn said. "It's so good to see you again."

Valentina hugged the other woman. "I missed you, too." And worse yet, she'd missed Cash. So damn much…

The past three years had been so hard, not knowing if she'd been doing the right thing, worried that she was cheating him and his daughters of the relationship they'd deserved to have. She hadn't considered all the other people she'd cheated, too. "I'm sorry," she said to Ashlynn. "I should have told you all about the girls."

"We would have been there for you," Ashlynn said. "Mom would probably have even moved back to New York to have a relationship with her grandbabies."

Valentina flinched as all the guilt and regret came over her.

"But we all understand," Ashlynn continued. "We know what Cash is like when he's working a case, how it consumes him. We know that you had your reasons for divorcing him."

"He was the one who served me," Valentina said. "I just wanted some space, moved in here to think…" She stared at the condo, remembering how empty it had felt without her grandparents here and especially without Cash here.

Ashlynn cursed. "Just goes to show what idiots guys are. I know he loved you. Loves you. I don't think he ever stopped. And when he got that text about you…" She shuddered. "From that sick serial killer…"

"After how you all lost your dad to one, I can understand how it would upset him."

"It upset him because it mentioned you," she said.

"Have you received one?" Valentina wondered.

Ashlynn shook her head. "And I sure as hell hope that I don't. But then it might give me another shot at tracing it back to the son of a bitch. He's good, though. He's smart."

Maybe too smart to get caught. Ashlynn didn't say it, but it was clear that the tech expert was worried about it. And she was worried about her brothers, too.

With another hug, she quickly left. And Valentina went back to the window to study those flashing lights and worry that it had been a trick, another way to draw Cash into danger.

Like the danger he'd been in the night before when that gunman had fired so many shots at him…

He'd gotten lucky in that only one had hit him and then only grazed him. Would his luck hold out if the killer came after him again?

If he was coming after him now?

Chapter 17

He had his orders to follow. He'd carried out the first part of it. There was one body...

One he hoped would never be found. Then there was the rest of it. Dispose of all possible evidence and every possible witness.

Sure. He'd disposed of what he'd needed to protect himself, but part of that was holding on to some insurance, because he dealt with people he couldn't trust. And he'd learned how to protect himself.

He hadn't counted on the witnesses that there'd been to that first part of his order, and while nobody might take them seriously at the moment, when they got older...

They were an unknown, a threat he had to eliminate. It wasn't just his reputation on the line anymore. It was his life. The person who'd hired him wasn't someone you could let down without consequences, which was another reason for that insurance he'd taken out.

The person who'd hired him was a killer and would have no qualms about killing him. Hell, even if he finished his assignment, he was liable to die because just like those little witnesses to his crime, he was a threat.

He needed to act fast and go underground again. But he could only go underground after those kids were dead.

And that woman…

They had to die if he had any chance of living himself.

The sounds of the rides and the flashing lights had Cash on edge. He wasn't worried about the killer standing out there somewhere beyond the lights and crime scene tape, hiding in the shadows. Cash *hoped* the Landmark Killer was there.

And not back at Valentina's building.

That was where Cash wanted to be. With the girls. Reading them the story they'd wanted him to read. Watching over them as they slept, keeping them safe.

And Valentina…

His pulse quickened just thinking about her. But that look on her face when he'd left her to deal on her own with the crying kids… He'd probably confirmed her every fear about him, about what kind of father he would be.

One who disappointed his kids.

Like, as a husband, he had disappointed her so many times. But if he didn't focus on his job, on stopping these serial killers, they would keep killing.

"He was shot to death," Patrick said.

"Will you run any ballistics from this scene against the ballistics from the parking garage?" Cash asked.

Patrick nodded, but his face was tense. So was Brennan's.

"You don't think he's the one who was shooting at me," Cash surmised.

"You don't match the profile," Patrick pointed out. And he pulled the sheet back from the victim's face. His blue eyes stared blankly up at them, shocked, as if he'd had no idea the bullets were coming. As if he'd been taken totally by surprise...

And he probably had been.

It was as if the Landmark Killer was invisible to these people, like he just appeared out of nowhere and killed. Only one of his victims had survived, and even that victim had been unable to give them very much information. Just a vague description that could have been anyone.

But they had a detailed description of all the victims. They all looked the same. Blue eyes. Blond hair. Thirties.

"Along with his ID, for an Eli Smith, I found this in his pocket." Patrick held out a see-through evidence bag containing a note. The lights from the Cyclone flashed a myriad of colors across the words:

*Until the brilliant and beautiful Maeve O'Leary is
freed, I will kill in her honor and name. MAEVE
down. O up.*

"But why here?" Cash asked. "Why so close to
Valentina's?" He glanced over his shoulder, and he
could see her high-rise building. He could probably
even see which window was hers. Was she there?
Watching for him?

Or was she still with the girls, trying to settle
them down? Soothe their tears?

She'd had to do that alone for the past nearly three
years. She knew what she was doing. Why did Cash
feel so guilty about leaving her?

And not just now but for all the other times he'd
left her during their marriage. When he'd gone out
when someone else could have taken the trip or handled the assignment…

"He's messing with us," Brennan said, his voice
gruff with irritation. "That article in the *New York
Wire.* The texts. And these damn notes. He knows
nobody is going to free Maeve O'Leary."

"So he's killing then for no real reason," Cash
said. "Why couldn't he be the one going after Valentina and the girls?"

"The car, for one thing," Patrick said. "Stealing
it right before using it to try to run them down. That
felt like a heat of the moment thing." He pointed to
the body lying on the ground. "This was thought out.
The victim and the location specifically chosen. The
guy going after you doesn't seem like a serial killer."

"But he's a professional of some sort," Cash said.

"That's what you and Ashlynn thought after finding the vehicle burned up."

Patrick nodded.

And Brennan reminded him, "We all make enemies."

Even Valentina…

Or the girls?

He nearly laughed at the thought of any of those three making someone angry enough to want them killed. So it had to be about him.

Maybe he shouldn't go back to her. To them.

Maybe he should let other officers protect them. Or hire a bodyguard for them. Maybe they would be safer without him in their lives. But then he remembered the girls' tears, and he ached to be with them now, holding them, reading to them. And after they fell asleep, he could be with Valentina like he'd been the night before, in her bed, with her in his arms.

He'd been a fool to leave them, especially if that was what someone had been waiting for. For him to leave them alone and unprotected.

But they weren't. Officers were there. And Ashlynn had even texted him that she was stopping by to talk to Valentina about her missing friend.

They were safe.

He was the one in danger of falling so hard for his family that he wouldn't be able to leave them ever again. And then more people would die like poor Eli Smith who probably had a family of his own, kids and a wife that he would never see again, just as Cash's dad had never been able to see his family again.

* * *

So much time had passed since Cash had left for the crime scene at Luna Park, Valentina had begun to suspect he was never coming back.

That might be for the best, so the girls got over him, so she got over him...

But she didn't know if he'd decided that he wasn't coming back or if someone else had decided for him. She was so worried about him. Was he okay?

Had that killing happened so close to her place just to lure Cash out there? So that he could kill him?

Or were she and the girls the targets now? That was how it had felt that day on the street for certain. Nobody could have known that Cash would show up when he had, that he was coming out to check on them.

If he hadn't...

She shuddered to think about what could have happened. She hadn't noticed that car coming at them until she'd already pushed the stroller into the street. If not for Cash knocking them back, out of the way, they could have been seriously hurt or worse.

Just like in the parking garage.

Cash had been out that day, meeting with his team, and nobody had taken any shots at him when he'd left on his own. Or when he'd returned on his own.

It wasn't until she and the girls had been with him that the gunshots had been fired. And while Cash was the one who'd been hit, he had been standing in front of them. Protecting them...

That was when and how he'd been hurt. So hopefully he was safe now, out there with his team.

What about her and the girls?

Instead of trying to sleep in her bed, the bed in which she and Cash had made love what seemed such a short time ago, she'd curled up on the couch. Not that she could relax or fall asleep.

But it put her between the door and the girls' bedroom. No matter who stood outside in the hall guarding them, she was guarding them, too. She wouldn't let anything happen to her girls, wouldn't let the danger touch them any more than it already had, that had them talking about bad guys and guns.

She felt their innocence slipping away from them as the danger hovered over them. When would it be safe for them to go back to their normal lives? Their routine?

Or was she being naive to think that anything could ever be the same again? That she would ever be the same again?

The doorknob rattled as if someone was messing with the lock, and she shot up from the couch, trembling with fear and anger. Anybody trying to get into the condo, to her girls, was going to have to go through her first.

She didn't have a gun, though. Thank God. With the girls' sudden fascination with them, she didn't like Cash even having his in the house, though he was good about keeping it out of their sight and reach.

Because she didn't have a gun, Valentina had to

scramble to find another weapon, something to protect her and the girls from danger. To keep them safe.

She rushed toward the kitchen and reached for the knife block. But a knife could be easily wrested away from her, if the intruder was bigger, stronger.

So she grabbed the cast-iron frying pan that hung from the copper hook over the island. It was heavy, unlike the teal ones that had hung beside it. Clasping the handle, she hurried back toward the door. The knob had stopped rattling for a moment as if the person was struggling to unlock it.

Cash had a key, so he would have opened the door already if it was him. He probably would have called out to her first, too. So it wasn't Cash trying to get in.

Who was?

What had happened to the officer stationed outside the door? Valentina wished now that she had asked Ashlynn to stay at least until Cash got back, but the FBI tech didn't carry a gun. Ashlynn wouldn't have been able to protect them like Cash had that day.

Where was Cash now? When she needed him?

Was he still at work on this case, chasing a killer while that killer was out there in the hall, trying to get to her and the girls?

Chapter 18

That damn neighbor was lurking around again. Despite how late it was, Blake Highland was the first thing Cash saw when he stepped off the elevator. As usual he was loitering outside Valentina's door.

When was he going to get the clue that she wasn't interested? That she didn't need him?

She hadn't even needed Cash the past three years. She'd gone through her pregnancy and the first few years of the twins' lives without any help from him. Financial or emotional.

She was strong and independent. So much so that Cash was surprised she'd let him stay this past week, that she hadn't tossed him out like she probably should have. But she loved their daughters more than she resented him, and she was willing to do anything to protect them.

Even put up with him.

But she'd done more than that the night before. They'd made love with all the passion they'd always had. Maybe even more because it had been so long. Too damn long since he'd been with her, inside her, part of her...

He had missed her so much these past three years and, somehow just these past few hours that he'd spent at the crime scene with the rest of his unit, he'd missed her even more. Clearly he shouldn't have stayed away so long since Blake Highland had taken it upon himself to hover around outside again.

Thankfully the officer was still at the door. A young woman in uniform, and Cash realized what Blake was doing here, flirting with the female officer. Instead of getting rid of the guy, she was smiling at him and leaning back against the door, so distracted that she didn't notice Cash approaching until he cleared his throat.

Then she jerked away from the door while Blake turned and glared at him, as if he was the intruder. When he reached for his shield, showing his badge, the officer touched her holster but didn't draw her weapon. Cash would have felt better if she had pointed her gun at him, at least until she'd seen that he was pulling out a badge and not his own gun. She wasn't the officer who'd been here when he'd left for Luna Park. She must have replaced the other female officer.

"Special Agent Colton," she said as her face flushed. "I was sent here to relieve the other officer and guard the door, but I wasn't told anything else. I didn't realize the FBI was involved in whatever is going on here…"

"That's my family in there," he said, staring hard at Blake Highland.

The guy smirked, his glassy eyes glinting with resentment. "Wouldn't have known it these past few years. Never been around till now…"

Cash was not about to defend or explain himself to this guy. "What are you doing around?" he asked Highland. "It's late. Why are you loitering outside my wife's door?"

The female officer's face flushed a deeper shade of red. She was young and inexperienced, so Cash wouldn't judge her too harshly for letting the guy distract her. But he also wouldn't trust her again to protect his family.

Hell, he really could only trust himself at this point. And Dave. Hell, maybe Dave was the better choice to keep them safe, but he'd been called out to Luna Park, too, since the body had been found in his precinct.

Basically in Valentina's backyard…

Why?

Cash turned toward Blake again. "What's your deal, Highland? You're hanging around all the time but you didn't notice that shooter in the garage last night?" Or had it been two nights ago? It was probably closer to morning than night right now.

"I wasn't in the garage," the man replied. "I asked you when you first turned up around here what was going on, if the rest of the building was in danger. You said we weren't and then that shooting happened in the garage. Innocent bystanders could have been hit. Killed. I'd say we are in danger. That having your family here is a risk to the rest of us."

"If you're so scared, what are you doing hanging around outside Valentina's door all the time?" Cash challenged his claim.

"I still care about her," Blake said, "I want to make sure she and those kids are safe."

The officer tensed even more, and now she glared at Blake, maybe realizing that his interest hadn't really been in her. The guy was pretty obsessed with Valentina. Obsessed enough to try to hurt her or the girls? For what reason? To scare her into *his* arms? Or out of anger and jealousy because she'd never given him a chance?

"I don't trust you, Highland," he admitted. "You have a stalking charge against you already. Want me to add another one to it?"

Now the officer gasped, probably realizing that she'd failed miserably at her job of guarding the door.

"You can leave now, Officer," he dismissed her.

"But, sir, I—"

"I've got this now," he assured her. "I will protect my family."

She glanced from him to Blake, who'd not slunk back to his apartment yet. Just how much had he had to drink? Enough to make him try something stupid?

Cash almost hoped he would, so that he would have a reason to arrest the guy and keep him away from Valentina.

The officer hurried off to the elevator, leaving Cash alone with the drunk neighbor.

"Your family," the guy said with a derisive snort. "You don't deserve or appreciate them."

Cash was tired. Tired from the shooting and then the long day and night, tired of chasing serial killers like the Landmark Killer who thought taking lives was some kind of sick game. And he was tired of this guy.

"Get the hell out of here," Cash advised him. "Before I arrest you."

"On what charge?" Blake asked. "And if you're going to do it without cause, I might just give you cause…" And he tightened his hands into fists, as if he was going to lunge at Cash.

As if he was going to fight him for Valentina.

Because he wanted her or because he wanted to hurt her?

Valentina had been standing against the wall for a while, listening to the deep rumble of voices in the hall. Was that Cash? Or someone else?

The officer?

She couldn't tell who was out there or what was going on. A tussle?

There were a few grunts. An expletive.

Then silence. Several long moments of silence. She

should have grabbed her cell phone, should have called 9-1-1 for backup for the officer.

For herself…

But she didn't see her phone on the couch; it must have dropped between the cushions. And in the time she took to find it, the intruder could get through that door, could get inside and get to the girls.

Fury replaced her fear, coursing through her, making her strong. Making her brave.

For them.

She had to protect them. So she gripped the frying pan so tightly that her fingers tingled from the effort. And when the lock rattled again, the dead bolt turning, she was ready. She'd shut off the lights, so that the intruder wouldn't see her in the shadows. But light from the hallway outside the door spilled into the room, blinding her for a moment so that she couldn't see who stood in the doorway, just the height and broadness of the shadow looming over her.

She stepped away from the wall and swung. The frying pan connected with a hard body with such force that Valentina lost her grip on it, and the heavy cast-iron skillet dropped to the floor with a resounding clang. That clang echoed the curse and grunt of pain from the shadow.

And she recognized that voice…too late.

She'd hit Cash.

"Are you okay?" she asked with alarm. What if she'd hit his wounded arm?

Before he could answer her, screams rang out

from the little girls' bedroom. Either they'd awakened with nightmares like they had a couple of times, or that loud clang and curse had awakened them.

And scared them.

All she'd wanted to do was protect them, but she'd made the situation worse, just as she had when she'd kept her pregnancy and their daughters secret from Cash and his family. Guilt and regret overwhelmed her.

"I'm coming," she called out to them. Then she turned back to Cash. "Are you okay?"

He closed the door behind him, shutting out the light from the hall, plunging them back into darkness.

And the girls screamed louder, as if they were closer or more frightened. Maybe they'd left their beds to find her, and they'd come into the living room just as it had gone dark again. They had been afraid of the dark even before all the bad things started happening.

The car nearly running them down.

The gunshots in the garage.

This, though, was her fault. And when the lights suddenly came on, she saw just how badly she'd screwed up when she saw the red mark on Cash's jaw. She had hurt him.

Chapter 19

Cash had stepped out of the chaos in the hall, the altercation with that idiot Highland, into the chaos inside the condo. The blow…

The screams.

And now the tears.

The little girls were crying, and tears glistened in Valentina's eyes, too. "I'm sorry," she said. "I didn't know it was you."

"Are you sure?" he asked, but he was just teasing. "I was gone longer than I thought I would be."

"I wouldn't hurt you," she said, and she reached out to touch his jaw. "Not purposely…"

"You didn't do this," he assured her. Highland had been drunk enough to hit him, and wanting a reason to hit him back, Cash had let him. He regretted that now since Valentina and the girls were so upset. He turned toward their daughters. "Hey, hey, you two, what's with all the tears? Everything's fine."

"Bang, bang," Ana sobbed. "Bang, bang…"

"It wasn't a gun," Valentina assured them. And she picked up the frying pan that had dropped to the floor. "It was this. That's what the noise was that woke you up."

"Bang, bang," Ana insisted.

"No, nobody was shooting," she said.

But that wasn't true. Earlier tonight someone had been shooting: the Landmark Killer. And a man had lost his life because of that. His family had lost someone they'd loved just like Cash and his mom and siblings had lost his dad so long ago. It wasn't fair.

That was why he'd chosen the job he had, why Brennan had worked so hard to get their special unit established so that they could focus solely on serial killers.

And that was what Cash had done all these years to the exclusion of everything else. Even the woman he'd loved…

The woman he still loved, if he was honest with himself. While he could be honest with himself, he didn't dare be honest with her, not when he was probably the reason she and the girls were in danger.

Why the girls were so scared.

Now tears stung his eyes, tears of regret that the darkness of his world had touched the lightness and innocence of theirs. Maybe Valentina had been right to never tell him about them, to never want him to be part of their lives.

But it was too late now. He couldn't undo what had been done; all he could do was try to keep them safe from any more darkness and danger.

"You don't have any reason to be afraid," he told them as he scooped them both up in his arms. He flinched a little at the ache in his shoulder, the one Valentina had whacked with the frying pan.

She was so fierce. So unbelievably brave and protective. It was no wonder he'd fallen for her all over again. But just like before, he knew she deserved better than him as a husband and as a father for her kids.

"I will keep you safe," he promised, and he hoped it was a promise he could keep. He glanced at Valentina and saw how her brow furrowed with concern. Obviously she didn't think he could keep it any more than he'd kept the promises he'd made her on their wedding day.

While her lips pursed, as if she wanted to say something, she didn't. She just carried that frying pan into the kitchen and set it in the sink.

He focused on the little girls, who snuggled against him, sniffling and shaking yet. "Let's read that story you wanted me to read," he suggested, trying to distract them from their fears.

He wished he could distract himself from his fear that something would happen to them, and he wouldn't be able to protect them like he'd promised.

Valentina was a mess of guilt and concern and... love. She loved her daughters so much, but she was also falling hard all over again for the man who cuddled with them in their beds, beds which he'd pulled close enough together so he could span the distance and lie between them, reading the story to them that Valentina had read so many times before.

They needed new books. But after what had happened in the garage the night before, she was afraid to take them out, afraid to put them in danger again.

Cash had vowed to keep them safe, but was that even a promise he could make, let alone keep? Finally they fell back to sleep, their eyes closed, their little bodies relaxed. They believed him, believed that he would protect them from the bad guys.

But Valentina saw how that red mark on his jaw was darkening to a bruise. If she hadn't done that with the frying pan, then someone else had. A bad guy from whom he hadn't protected himself?

He gently eased Ana from his right arm and then Luci from his left, and as he did, he flinched. Was he in pain from the bullet wound or from where she'd struck him?

"Are you okay?" she asked in a whisper.

He didn't answer her until he got away from their beds, squeezing sideways through the narrow space he'd left between them, and into the hall. "I'm fine," he said.

"Liar," she accused him, and she brushed her fingertips along his jaw. "You need an ice pack."

"It's fine."

"What happened?" she asked, her heart beating fast with concern. "Was it a trap? The crime scene at Luna Park?"

He released a heavy sigh. "Not for me. There was another victim, matching the description of the other ones, with a note from the Landmark Killer in his pocket."

She gasped.

"I shouldn't have shared that with you."

"I won't tell anyone," she assured him. She didn't want to think about a killer, much less talk about him. And she knew that psychopaths like that sometimes killed for the attention, for the fame.

He sighed again. "I'm sure it'll get out somehow, and if it doesn't, the Landmark Killer will make sure that it does, just like he got that article out about my dad." His voice cracked on that; the pain must have still been fresh all these years later.

Or maybe that article had made it fresh again. Even before she'd read that, Valentina had known that his dad was the reason that Cash did what he did, pursuing serial killers. And that was the reason that she had never asked him to leave his job, to quit doing what he felt he had to do; she'd just asked that he not let it consume him and destroy them.

He hadn't been able to keep that promise to her. She hoped he could keep the one he'd made to their daughters.

"If this didn't happen at the crime scene, where did it happen?" she asked, wondering about that mark on his jaw, hoping that she hadn't caused it with the frying pan despite his assurances that she hadn't.

"Hallway," he said.

She sucked in a breath. So she had been right to

worry. "You were attacked in the hallway? Someone was out there trying to get in?"

"Your damn neighbor again," Cash said, his voice lowering to a growl.

"Blake Highland attacked you? He was the one trying to get inside?"

Cash sighed now. "I don't know if he was trying to get in or just trying to get a rise out of me."

"But you're the one who got hit," she said. "Did you have the officer arrest him?"

He shook his head. "I already let the young officer go," he said. "And Highland wasn't worth the paperwork. He's on notice now. He knows we've checked out his record."

"Record…"

"Couple driving under the influence convictions and a stalking charge," Cash said.

She shivered with the realization that her instincts about the guy had been right. She hadn't trusted him and apparently with good reason.

"You're cold," Cash said. "You need to go back to bed, too."

"I wasn't in bed yet," she said.

"It's late."

"I was scared," she admitted.

"It didn't show. You were fierce with that frying pan," he remarked, his mouth curving into a grin. And he touched his shoulder now and grimaced.

"I did hit you," she said. "I'm sorry. I didn't know it was you. I heard someone messing with the door, and I was worried."

"You gave me the keys when I left," he reminded her. "So I could let myself in without waking you up." He stepped closer now and touched her cheek, cupping it in his palm. "But I can see that you never went to sleep."

"I couldn't," she said. "I was worried about you, too, that it was a trap to get you out of here."

"I was worried about that, too," he said. "That it might have been a trick to lure me away from you, so someone could try to hurt you and the girls again."

"Why?" she asked. "Why come after us to get to you? And why would he even want to get to you? Are you that close to catching him?"

He grimaced again, but it seemed to be with frustration, not pain. "I wish. While we've narrowed it down to six possible suspects, the one I was assigned to investigate has alibis. It's not him. So I pose no threat to this killer. I have no idea why he threatened you."

"But did he?" she asked. "You showed me that text. He just mentioned me, just like he mentioned your dad. He didn't threaten to hurt me. He just called me sad." And he hadn't been wrong. Whenever she'd thought of Cash over the years, she had gotten sad.

But how had he known that?

Had he been watching her?

"Brennan doesn't think it's the Landmark Killer who's come after you. He thinks he just sends these texts to mess with us," Cash admitted.

"Is that what you think now?" she asked. "You

don't believe anymore that he's the one who tried to run down me and the girls? Who shot at us in the parking garage?"

He shrugged and pushed a slightly shaky hand through his overly long hair. "I don't know..."

"I feel like it has something to do with Mrs. Miller," she admitted. "The timing of her disappearing and when all that started happening to me and the girls, it seems like too great a coincidence."

He released a soft breath and his shoulders sagged slightly. "I hope it's not because of me. I hope that I haven't brought this evil into your lives."

She could see how much that bothered him. She took his hand and tugged him toward her bedroom. "It's not your fault that there's evil in the world, Cash," she said. "And it's not your responsibility to stop it all by yourself."

She'd told him that so many times during their marriage. That he didn't have to act as if he was the only one who could stop the serial killers. He had a team that all worked together toward that goal, and there were others in law enforcement who fought like they did, who enforced justice, who caught the killers.

"The girls shouldn't have been your responsibility all on your own either," he said. "I should have been helping you, financially and..."

"You said you didn't want a family," she said when he trailed off. What had he left unsaid? What had he thought she needed besides financial support? Him? Unfortunately she had, but she hadn't thought he wanted her. "You didn't want *this*. Didn't want them. I didn't want to force another responsibility onto you."

"Valentina," he murmured, his voice gruff with frustration and remorse. Then he reached out and pulled her into his arms, holding her close. His long body shuddered against hers. "There are so many things I want to ask you. So many promises I want to make."

"Don't," she said. "Don't make promises you can't keep. Not to me and not to the girls."

He flinched as if she'd hit him with that frying pan again. "I know I disappointed you before. And I don't want to disappoint them."

"I already told you that you can't take responsibility for everything," she reminded him. "You can't take complete responsibility for our safety. You can't be with us 24/7. I have to get back to work. The girls need to get back to their day care, back to their routine."

"I know. I just wish…"

"What?" she asked.

"That we could stay here in this little safe bubble, at least for a little while longer."

But it wasn't safe. Not for her. She was falling for him all over again, and that was putting her heart in danger. But for the moment, for what was left of the night, she didn't want to worry about it.

So she tugged him the rest of the way into her bedroom and closed the door behind them, locking it in case the girls woke up again. She would hear them if they tried to get in or if they called out from their room. But for the moment she didn't want to be just a mother.

She wanted to be a woman, too. And nobody had ever made her more aware of her sexuality than Cash. He must have realized what she wanted, because he began to undress her, slowly unbuttoning her blouse. And every inch of skin he bared, he kissed and caressed.

Her knees began to shake, threatening to fold beneath her. As if he knew, he lifted and carried her to the bed. Then he pulled off her yoga pants and underwear, and he stroked and touched her everywhere.

Heat streaked through her, and she throbbed as the tension built inside her. She needed a release. She needed Cash. She reached out toward him, trying to tug him down with her.

But he stepped back instead, and then he stripped off his clothes. Blood had seeped through the bandage on his right arm, as if his stitches had reopened.

She worried that she'd done that with the frying pan, but then she saw the angry red mark on his left shoulder. She could have hit his head or neck with as close as she'd come. She could have seriously injured him. Guilt gripped her.

Finally, naked, he joined her on the bed.

She reached out and touched his shoulder. "I'm so sorry."

"I'm not," he said. "I'm damn impressed. You're so strong, Valentina. So resourceful."

She'd had to be, loving him like she had and losing him, but she didn't want to make him feel any guiltier than he already did.

So instead of talking, she pushed him onto his back, and with her mouth and her hands, she showed him how resourceful she could be.

His body tensed and shuddered, sweat beading on his brow. "You're torturing me, Valentina. I need you." Then he lifted her up until she straddled him, and he eased inside her.

She was on top, in charge, so she set the pace, teasing him with slow rocking movements. He teased her back, cupping her breasts in his hands, rubbing her nipples between his thumbs and index fingers.

She arched her neck and swallowed the moan bubbling up the back of her throat. And that pressure that built inside her became unbearable. Then he moved his hands to her hips, clutching them as he thrust.

And the pressure broke as an orgasm shuddered through her. But he kept moving and she kept coming until finally his body tensed and pulsed beneath her. He came, and she dropped onto his chest, which heaved with his pants for breath. His heart pounded as fast and frantically as hers did and she melted against him, feeling boneless with satisfaction.

If only this could last…

If only they could stay in this bubble forever… that was what she wanted. But she knew they'd have to get back to the real world soon, the world that at the moment was filled with danger for all of them.

Chapter 20

He couldn't wait around for them to come out again. He had to finish up this assignment and get the hell out of Brooklyn before this assignment finished him.

He had to get rid of them because he figured it was only a matter of time before someone figured out what those girls had seen and what he'd done. And he was as much of a loose end to the man who'd hired him as those girls were to him…

At least he'd gotten some insurance. If he didn't make it out of this assignment alive, there would be consequences for a lot of other people. If the right person knew where to look…

Like he knew where to look for that damn loose end he'd left dangling. He had to pluck it off, had to burn them up like he had that car. And like he should have the body. But it wouldn't be found. At least he hoped, since he wasn't even sure where it was now himself.

But he knew where *they* were. He just had to figure out a way to get them out. So he could kill them all.

Cash had to leave them again. He hated doing it, especially as it was getting close to night again, but when Valentina had learned that Ashlynn got one of those texts, she'd insisted he support his sister.

Before he left, Cash made sure that Dave was the one watching the door this time; he didn't trust anyone else to protect his family. His family...

He hadn't wanted one, just as Valentina kept reminding him, but now that he had them, he couldn't imagine his life without them.

That afternoon, before Ashlynn had let him and the others in the unit know about her text, Cash had been FaceTiming his mom in Florida, introducing her to his daughters, her granddaughters. Mom had cried, and Valentina had, too, with guilt for keeping their daughters from the Colton family.

He knew why she'd done it, though, because she hadn't trusted him not to hurt and disappoint the girls like he had her. His mother must have known as well, because she'd assured Valentina that she understood and that she just wished she could have been there for her and the girls. And she'd promised that she would be from now on.

Cash knew that his mother would keep her promise. She always did. Could he keep the promises he'd made to the girls, though?

Before disconnecting the call with his mom, he'd spoken to her alone for a moment. And she'd cried harder than she had over meeting her granddaughters. "This was what I wanted for you, Cash, for you and Valentina," she said. "I wanted you to build a future, to enjoy the present and to let go of the past."

"Mom—"

She'd interrupted him with a laugh, as if she'd known what he was about to say. "I know that probably sounds hypocritical coming from me. But it's not like I didn't try to move on after your father died. I just never found anyone I loved like I loved him. He was my soulmate. Like I think Valentina is yours. Don't let her go a second time, Cash. Don't put your work before her again."

That was good advice, advice he'd had to ignore when just an hour or so after that call ended, he learned about Ashlynn's text.

"Go," Valentina had insisted.

And he'd felt a twinge uneasy, as if she wanted to get rid of him, as if she needed some space. They'd made love again the night before, but just like the last time, when he'd awakened, she was already up.

It wasn't because the girls had awakened her, either, because he'd found her alone in the kitchen, looking pensive as she sipped a cup of coffee. "You okay?" he had asked.

"I just keep thinking about Mrs. Miller." She was worried about her friend, and now she was worried about his sister. Valentina was such a caring person, such a loving protective mother.

And as a wife, she really hadn't asked for much from him. She hadn't wanted him to quit his job, just strike a better balance between his professional life and his personal life. He hadn't been able to figure out how to do that. Maybe if he'd tried harder...

But he'd always applied that attitude to cases. If they tried harder, they could catch the killer. They had to...because the Landmark Killer was too damn close now, to Valentina and the girls as well as the rest of Cash's family.

"You okay?" Brennan now asked the same question Cash had posed to Valentina that morning, drawing Cash out of his thoughts and back to the present and that small hotel suite he'd rented again.

Brennan and Patrick had been there when Cash had arrived. But Ashlynn...

"I'm just worried," Cash admitted. About all his family. Even though Dave was watching the door, he had a really bad feeling about leaving Valentina and the girls alone. After the attempt in the parking garage, there was no doubt that the shooter knew where they lived. How had he even gotten into the structure? Was he a resident?

"What happened to your face?" Patrick asked, pointing to the bruise on Cash's jaw. "You didn't have that last night at the crime scene."

"I had a small altercation with one of Valentina's neighbors," Cash admitted.

"A suspect in the parking garage shooting?" Patrick asked. "It would make sense to be someone in the building. Otherwise I don't know how he would have gotten in."

"It would make sense," Cash said. "But I don't think the guy would try to hurt her and the girls." Who would? Who was that big a monster? The Landmark Killer…

"He just wanted to hurt you?" Patrick asked with an arched eyebrow.

"He was drunk and goading me," Cash said. "Probably trying to get me banned from the building."

"So you let him hit you first," Brennan said.

He shrugged. "I don't want Valentina to get in trouble with the condo board." She loved that place, had had some of her happiest childhood moments in that condo with her grandparents. He didn't want to take that away from her, just as three years ago he hadn't wanted to take away her dream of having a family someday.

A knock rattled the door, and Brennan opened it to Ashlynn. "Where have you been?" he asked. "We've been worrying about you."

Ashlynn looked worried, too, her face a bit pale, and her hand trembled slightly as she reached out to close and lock the door behind her. "I'm just mad," she insisted. "I'm sick of this guy playing games with us."

"Show us the text," Patrick said.

She held out her cell, and they all passed it around. Brennan read it first and cursed, then handed the phone to Cash.

Your poor murdered daddy wouldn't be very proud of how little you've accomplished in HIS name. Should you even be alive yourself?

This wasn't as innocuous as the texts to Sinead and Brennan and him had been. This wasn't just a taunt; it was clearly a threat.

"Son of a bitch," he muttered, and as he passed the phone to Patrick, his hand shook a little with fury and fear for his sister.

Patrick read it and closed his eyes for a moment before focusing on Ashlynn again. "I assume this is also untraceable?"

She nodded. "I tried."

"Well, you're done," Brennan said. "You're off the case and off to a safe house. That is a blatant threat."

Ashlynn shook her head. "He's not scaring me off this case."

"We'll work harder, around the clock on it," Cash vowed. "We'll catch him." And once again he was making promises he might not be able to keep, promises that might make him break other promises…to his family.

But the Landmark Killer had blatantly threatened Ashlynn's life.

"You need to be in a safe house, protected," Brennan insisted. "Preferably a safe house far away from New York."

That was where Cash was going to have to put Valentina and the girls, somewhere the shooter wouldn't be able to find them. The Landmark Killer? Or someone else?

"I am leaving town," Ashlynn said. And she turned slightly to show the backpack she carried. "I've got my phones and my laptop. And I've a got a lead I need to follow."

"You're not a special agent," Brennan reminded her. "You're our tech expert."

"Yeah, so I know how to go completely off the grid," she assured him. "Nobody will be able to track me down. I'll be safe."

"What's the lead?" Cash asked. "Is it about Xander Washer?" He was the potential suspect she'd been assigned to investigate.

"I thought he had alibis for the murders," Patrick said.

She shrugged. "Yeah, but I don't know. There's something fishy about them."

"We need to tell the director," Brennan said with a sigh.

"Let me check this out first," Ashlynn said. "And I'll let you know what I find." She turned toward Cash. "Speaking of finds, I think Valentina's friend turned up."

"Alive?" He hoped that was the case, that the woman had simply gone on an impromptu trip.

She shook her head.

He cursed, and that feeling he'd had that he shouldn't have left Valentina and the girls intensified. They were definitely in danger, and even if it didn't have anything to do with the Landmark Killer, someone was obviously still very determined to kill them.

* * *

Valentina was worried about a lot of things. One of them was that text that Ashlynn had received; she was worried about her. That was mainly why she'd encouraged Cash to go to that meeting with his siblings. She knew how close they all were, especially after their father's murder. Hopefully Ashlynn wasn't in danger.

Valentina was, of falling so hard for Cash that she wouldn't be able to get over him again. If she ever actually had.

That was another reason she'd been happy for Cash to leave for a while. So she could take a breath without inhaling the scent of him. So her pulse could slow to a normal rate. So she wasn't so aware of him that every nerve tingled.

But even with him gone, she couldn't stop thinking about him, about how they kept making love like they were making up for lost time. For three years…

Even though they'd been exhausted the past couple of nights, they hadn't been able to get enough. To love enough.

To feel enough.

But it wasn't just pleasure and attraction that she felt around him. There were so many other emotions.

That morning, while on that call with his mom, she'd felt so guilty about keeping the girls from the Colton side of their family. But his mom was right; she couldn't change the past. She could focus only on the future.

And she had to make sure that her girls had one.

Cash had promised to keep them safe, but was that possible with all the dangers in the world?

She couldn't worry about all of them, though, just that man with the gun. The bad man…

That was what the girls called him. But they'd talked about him and that gun even before the shooting that day. "Bang bang," she murmured.

"Bang bang," Ana repeated, and then she shuddered. The girls were on the couch, watching cartoons. With the parental controls Valentina had on the TV, she doubted they'd seen anything violent on that.

That they'd seen anything violent until that day someone had tried running them down. Then Cash had taken shots at the car, making the driver speed away. Saving them…

So he wasn't the bad man they'd talked about, the bad man that went bang bang.

"Did you see a bad man with a gun before that day Luci was sick?" she asked Ana.

Ana turned toward her, and her dark eyes were wide with fear.

Oh, my God…

She had seen something.

"What was it, sweetheart?" Valentina asked. "You can tell me."

"Tell her bang bang," Luci advised her twin. "And Sparky falled down."

"Sparky…"

Oh, my God, Valentina repeated in her head. Sparky was what they'd called Mrs. Miller because of all her jewelry. "You saw the lady from the library?" she asked them both. "The one with all the pretty sparkling rings and necklaces?"

Luci shook her head and pointed at Ana. "She saw Sparky...by the garbage with the bad man."

Tears brimmed in Ana's dark eyes, and when she nodded, the tears spilled over and trailed down her face. "Bad man go bang bang and Sparky falled down..."

Her little girl had witnessed a mugging or worse yet, maybe a murder, since Mrs. Miller had gone missing. And then Valentina remembered their walk home from the library that day, how she'd been distracted, so distracted that she'd been startled when she'd heard a car backfire.

But what if it hadn't been a car?

What if it had been the bang bang that the girls kept talking about?

"Where Sparky at?" Ana asked. "In the garbage?"

Had the man thrown Mrs. Miller into a dumpster? Valentina's heart pounded heavy with dread and fear. And she hated that her baby girl had witnessed such an atrocity. She wrapped her arm around Ana, holding the little girl's trembling body close to her side as she reached for her cell.

She had to call Cash, had to let him know what Ana had said, what she had witnessed. Luci had been on the street side of the stroller, so Ana would have had just the view of buildings and...

Maybe an alley between them, where the dumpsters would have been. That had happened over a week ago, though, so the dumpster would have been emptied. And Mrs. Miller...

Tears stung her own eyes as she considered what might have happened to the older woman. She'd been so elegant, so glamorous, like old Hollywood royalty.

"Daddy," Ana murmured. "I want Daddy."

Valentina nodded. She wanted him, too, and wished now that she wouldn't have encouraged him to leave. Because she had a horrible feeling that the bad man had seen Ana, too, and that was why that car had come at them.

And then the shooter in the garage...

He must have followed them back here, or maybe he'd asked around about them and learned where they lived. Everybody at the library and the day care knew.

"I'm calling Daddy now," Valentina said. And she pulled up the contact for his cell but her call went directly to his voice mail. "Cash, I think we figured out what's going on. That Ana saw something..."

"The bad man!" the little girl cried. "The bad man!"

"He's not here," Valentina said. "You're safe." Then she turned her attention back to her cell. "She saw what happened to Mrs. Miller, Cash. And that man must have seen her, too."

An alarm pealed out, and the lights in the condo blinked before going out along with the TV. The girls screamed.

"It's just the smoke alarm," she assured them. "Probably just the super testing it—"

But then someone pounded at the door. "Mrs. Colton, Mrs. Colton," Sergeant Percell called out to her, "there's smoke, and the alarm is going off."

She heard that; it was ringing in her ears. And the girls were covering theirs.

"We need to evacuate."

Valentina clicked off her cell and shoved it in her pocket. But she would need money to go someplace else, stay someplace else. So she rushed to her bedroom to grab her purse. And the girls went to their rooms. "We have to leave," she told them from the doorway. "Just take your favorite stuffed animals. The bear and the bunny."

They didn't have time to pack up more, not if there was a fire. And if there was a fire, while Valentina would hate to lose the condo, she would always have her memories of being there. It was the girls she wouldn't be able to handle losing. They mattered most.

Keeping them safe...

But she couldn't help thinking as she opened the door that this was a trap. That the bad man was behind this just like he was apparently behind Mrs. Miller's disappearance.

Was he going to try to make Valentina and the girls disappear like Mrs. Miller had?

Forever.

Chapter 21

Valentina had been right to be worried about her missing friend. Adelaide Stewart Miller had been murdered. Shot to death, and her body tossed in a dumpster. If not for a homeless man rummaging through that dumpster, her body might not have been found before the trash was collected. But he'd pulled her out along with her bag and the jewelry that had been left on her body.

It hadn't been a mugging. It must have been a hired hit.

"The ballistics match what we recovered at the parking garage," Patrick said, his cell pressed to his ear as one of his CSIs told him what their tests had confirmed.

The same man who'd killed the library patron had come after Valentina and the girls. But why?

"We're going through her laptop and other things, too," Patrick assured him.

"Why did it take so long for her body to turn up?" Cash asked. She'd been missing for more than a week.

"The homeless guy took her to his hiding place in the sewer through a manhole right in that alley. He thought he could save her. He'd once been a med student," Ashlynn relayed. "Another homeless person that he asked to help him stole some of her jewelry and hocked it. When local police tracked him down and questioned him, he said where she could be found."

Cash shuddered at the gruesome details he didn't want to share with Valentina. She'd really liked the older woman. But that wasn't reason enough for someone to go after her and the girls. Unless...

Bang bang...

Had one of the girls witnessed the shooting?

"What dumpster?" Cash asked Ashlynn. "Where did the homeless person find her?"

"Not far from the library where Valentina works."

"On her route home?"

Ashlynn nodded.

And Cash's stomach plummeted. He reached for his cell, remembering just then that they'd shut them off and taken out their batteries just in case the Landmark Killer tried to trace them while they were at the hotel. He had to wait until he was out of here to reattach his battery. "I have to go. I have to make sure they're okay."

He hugged Ashlynn. "Take care of yourself and stay off the grid, so this sick bastard…"

She chuckled. "Though I know it's hard for my brothers to accept, I can take care of myself," she said. "I'll be fine."

"You don't carry a gun," Brennan reminded her.

She tapped her temple. "I don't need it. I can outsmart him."

Could they, though? So far it seemed like the Landmark Killer had been ahead of them, that he knew them too well. "You need to be careful," Cash insisted.

She nodded. "I will. You, too." She touched his jaw. "Looks like you're in more danger than I am."

He shook his head. "I don't think it's me who's in danger." It was his family, and he needed to get back to them.

"Go," Brennan said.

He was already opening the door, already rushing out. He waited until he was in the parking lot before he put the battery back into his phone, and when he did, his screen lit up with a voice mail.

And when he played it…

His blood chilled. The girls had witnessed that older woman's murder. The bang bang. The bad man. They knew who he was, had seen him kill the woman.

That was why the killer had gone after them. He must not have kids or know kids that well, or he wouldn't have considered them much of a threat. At less than three years old, even if the prosecutor considered them credible witnesses, they probably would have been too scared or shy to testify against him.

But the man had tried to kill them not once but twice. And then Cash heard the alarm…

And he knew that the guy was going to try again. Right now.

The smoke was pungent and thick, so much so that it was hard for Valentina to see. It was thicker here in the stairwell that led down to the parking garage. The girls coughed and sputtered and burrowed their faces into her neck. She was carrying both of them while Sergeant Percell led the way down, his gun clasped in his hand.

Thankfully the girls couldn't see it, since he was ahead of them and they were snuggled so closely against her. Even with their faces against her, she could feel the tears streaming from their eyes and from hers. She didn't know if that was because of the smoke or the fear.

"The fire must be in the parking garage," Sergeant Percell remarked, his voice raspy, and he coughed. "We should go back up. Or get out on one of these floors and head to another stairwell."

She knew that was what they needed to do, especially because of how she could hear someone coming down from above, and the way their footsteps sounded on the stairs, almost stealthy, as if they were stalking them.

Because she and the girls had taken time to grab her purse and their favorite stuffed animals, they'd been behind everyone else exiting the building. And nobody had been behind them, that she'd noticed, until this moment.

"Now," she shouted at Percell. "Open the door to that floor!"

The fourth. They'd come down seven, and her legs and arms burned from carrying the girls and her own weight down so many flights.

Dave must have heard the urgency in her voice because he stopped and pushed open that door, but he paused before passing through it. First he glanced out into the hall then he looked back at her and the girls. Then he raised his gaze and the barrel of his gun above her. "Go! Go!" he shouted, and she knew he'd noticed what she had.

That they were not alone.

She ran down the last couple of steps and through the door he held open for her. And as it swung shut, she heard the gunshots coming from behind her.

The exit light at the end of the hall was the only thing glowing in the darkness and the smoke. She ran toward that as the girls cried in her arms. She had to get out of here, had to get to the street. This stairwell would bring her there and to safety if she could get there before the shooter got past Sergeant Percell. Dave.

He'd told her to call him Dave. He would do his best to stop the shooter, to protect them, and hopefully he would save himself, too. She liked the man. He was like Cash, intent on protecting them. So she knew he would probably give his life for theirs. Tears stung her eyes, and she hoped that he wouldn't have to, that he would survive.

But she had to focus on the girls now, on getting them to safety. She ran down the hall to the opposite stairwell, where that sign glowed faintly through the smoke. It hadn't been as thick, but now that the door had opened onto the floor, so much had billowed into it that it stung her eyes here, too, making it harder to see. She blinked to clear her vision, but the smoke remained like fog. The exit light beckoned through it, and she reached the other stairwell door and turned around to push it open with her back.

She glanced back at the other end of the hall, to the other stairwell. While the smoke was thick, she could tell that it was still closed, the hallway still empty behind her. Nobody had come out of the stairwell yet. Maybe Dave had held the shooter off.

Maybe the officer was okay. She couldn't check on him, though. Her girls still weren't safe.

"Mommy..." Luci murmured, her soft voice raspy.

She had to get them out of the smoke, too. Legs and arms burning, she started down the stairwell, keeping her balance by leaning against one wall, the handrail digging into her side. She'd made it down three flights when she heard the door slam open above them.

Dave would have called out, would have assured them that they were safe now. No assurances came. Just pounding footsteps...

He wasn't even trying to be stealthy anymore. He was just trying to catch them. To kill them...

She needed something. Some way to protect them, because she was worried that he would start shooting soon. And there was nowhere to hide in the stairwell.

She ran faster. Tripping on one step, she nearly dropped the girls. Pain shot through her ankle, and her arms ached. She had to let them go.

"Run," she told them. "Run to the bottom of the stairs and go out that door. Then run toward the lights. As fast as you can!"

"Mommy!" Luci protested.

She shook her head. "I'll be right behind you. Run toward the lights. Run to safety. Go!" And she gave them a little shove, propelling them ahead of her.

They looked back once. Then they grabbed each other's hands and ran ahead of her. She tried to run after them, ignoring the twinge in her ankle with every step she took. As she descended, she looked around, looking for something that could help her. That could protect her and the girls.

On the last landing, a fire extinguisher lay where someone had dropped it. She grabbed it up, and even though it was lighter than the girls, her arm hurt. She ached everywhere, but that discomfort was going to be nothing compared to the pain she would feel if something happened to her daughters. If she didn't do everything she could to try to save them, even give up her own life if she had to.

The door at the bottom of the stairs opened. And Ana must have hesitated, because she heard Luci say, "Mommy said to run. Run to the lights."

And the door slammed shut behind them. She

had just a few more steps to go, a few more, but he was close now. So close that the gun fired, a bullet striking off the concrete wall of the stairwell, close to her head. She ran down the last flight and pushed open that door to darkness.

Where were the lights? Where were her girls?

The only lights she could see were the lights from Luna Park, from the roller coaster and the Ferris wheel. And she could hear the music from the carousel...

Where were the girls?

Would they realize that they had come out the back of the building and they needed to circle around to the front entrance to where the fire trucks and police had to be? Those were the lights she'd wanted them to find and the help and protection that they needed right now.

That she needed right now...

She held the fire extinguisher yet. And instead of running around to the front or toward the lights, she shrank into the shadows and clasped her weapon tightly, uncertain how to use it in her defense.

Throw it at him? Wait until the shooter was close enough that she could hit him over the head with it? But if he was close enough...

The door opened again, and a dark shadow stepped out of it, that gun pointed out. Maybe toward her daughters, whom she couldn't see in the dark. What if he could? What if he was aiming that barrel at them now?

A mother's instinct to protect her babies raging

inside her, she swung the fire extinguisher at the arm holding the gun, whacking it harder than she had Cash with the frying pan. Or at least she hoped she had, because her life and her daughters' lives depended on it.

Chapter 22

Lights flashed around the high-rise from the fire trucks and emergency vehicles pulled up next to the building. So close that Cash couldn't get near it. He had to abandon his SUV down the street and run the rest of the way.

Smoke billowed out from the parking garage, acrid with the smell of burning rubber. Someone must have set a car on fire in the parking garage. Someone...

He knew damn well who'd done it. That son of a bitch who was after his wife and kids. Cash could only hope that he'd arrived in time to protect them.

To save them...

Residents stood around the parking lot, staring up at the building. Cash scanned the crowd, looking for the beautiful dark-haired woman and the two curly-haired little girls. But he caught not even a glimpse of them. Or of Dave...

Where the hell was Dave? Cash had tried calling him on his way to the condo, but the call had gone straight to Dave's voice mail, like the call Valentina had made to Cash. If only he'd been here...

He never should have left them. But Ashlynn was in danger, too. Ashlynn, while not a special agent, had been at the FBI so long that she knew how to take care of herself. Valentina was a librarian with such a soft, loving heart, unless she was protecting her children, like she had the night she'd hit him with the frying pan. Then she could be fierce.

But as fierce as she was, she couldn't stop someone with a gun, like the man who'd ambushed them in the parking garage a couple of nights ago. He must have come back through the parking garage, setting a car on fire first to flush out the residents. To flush out Cash's family.

He headed toward the parking garage now, but a crime scene was already set up, a tape stretching between two police vehicles, tied to their side mirrors. When he went to duck under the tape, an officer stepped up, hand on holster. "Sir, you have to stay back!"

He reached into his pocket, and the officer drew the weapon. "I'm FBI," he said. "Special Agent Cash Colton." He showed his shield. "What's going on?"

Because the officer wouldn't have been so on edge from just a fire...

"Shots fired," the officer said, then turned back as other officers and EMTs came out of the garage.

They carried a stretcher. Someone had been hurt. Or worse…

His heart pounding furiously with fear, Cash ducked under the tape and rushed over to the back of the ambulance where the EMTs were loading the stretcher. "Valentina?"

The body on the stretcher moved, but it was a male voice that called out to him. "Cash?"

"Dave!" Once the EMTs jumped into the ambulance, he could see his friend. The guy's face was pale and contorted with pain. Blood seeped from his shoulder and his leg. "You've been shot!"

"We have to get him to the hospital," a paramedic said as he reached for the doors, to pull them shut.

But Dave reached out, grasping the guy's arm. "Wait."

"Valentina? The girls?" Cash asked, his voice cracking with the fear overwhelming him.

"She heard him coming. She took the girls and ran toward the other stairwell."

But clearly Dave didn't know if they'd made it or not.

"I tried…" He coughed and sputtered.

"We gotta go now," the paramedic said, and he pulled the doors closed on Cash.

Before the ambulance even pulled away, Cash was running toward the building. A fireman blocked the way. "You can't go inside. There's too much smoke."

He flashed his shield again. "My kids and wife are in there."

The firefighter shook his head. "Our team checked the building. The shooting victim was the only one still inside."

Because he'd been unable to get out…

So maybe the girls had managed to escape. From the building or from the killer, too?

"I checked the crowd," he said. "I didn't see them."

"There are two fire exits, here, through the parking garage and the other at the opposite end, back side of the building," the fire fighter said. "Some people came out that way, less smoke."

So maybe they were back there, safe.

Cash ran toward that opposite end of the building, and the air was clearer, less smoke, less light, especially when he turned the corner. The building, without power, was dark, casting a giant shadow over whatever was behind it. A parking lot? A field?

He couldn't see anything. But he could hear someone grunting, someone breathing heavily…

Pulling out his gun and a flashlight, he shone it around the area, which was overgrown with weeds. And he saw the man with that damn hoodie pulled tight around his face, which was covered in a mask.

Cash raised his gun and squeezed the trigger. But the man ducked and ran deeper into the shadows. Cash started to follow him until a moan in the dark brought his attention back to where he'd first seen the man.

And now he saw the body lying on the ground, in the weeds. Valentina…

* * *

It had all happened so quickly. Her knocking that gun from the man's grasp, and when he'd crouched down to retrieve it, she had struck him again so hard that she'd lost her grip on the fire extinguisher. Then the man had reached out for her, closing his hands around her neck, cutting off her breath, her consciousness, her life…

No. She had to fight, had to stay alive to protect her babies. She kicked and punched and clawed until her hands were covered in blood.

Or was that because of a wound on the man?

Dave must have shot him. He was bleeding.

She could fight him off. But then he found the gun and pressed it to her head. When he pulled the trigger, it clicked. He'd already emptied it.

She thrashed harder, fighting to get away from him before he could reload, and he grabbed her neck again. His grip tightened, and everything started to go black inside her head as her lungs burned for air.

Then she heard another gunshot blast, close but yet muffled. Had he managed to reload his weapon? How? She could feel both hands wrapped around her neck.

Then the hands left her throat, and she gasped for air and fought for consciousness. She had to stop him. But when she swung her arms around, she didn't feel anything.

As if she was floating, floating away…floating into oblivion. Then she actually *was* floating, because someone lifted her from the ground.

"Valentina? Valentina?" Cash called to her, and he sounded as if he was far away even though those were his arms holding her, carrying her. "Where are the girls?" he asked.

And his question jarred her back into consciousness with the sudden rush of fear. She tensed and tried to wriggle away from him. "Wh…" Her voice was raspy, her throat burning, and not from the smoke. "Where…?"

"Where are they?" he finished the question for her. "I checked in the front. They're not there. Were the firefighters wrong? Are they still in there? Hiding?"

She shook her head. "No. They ran ahead. They got out…" She'd heard the door. But she hadn't seen them. "I told them to go…" Her voice trailed off, and she fought to clear her throat, but it was swelling. She swallowed hard, finding more saliva to continue speaking, "…toward the lights…"

"What lights?" he asked, glancing around.

"I…" She struggled to get out the words. "Police. Fire trucks…"

"But you can't see them from here," he murmured, and then he turned, with her still in his arms, toward the lights of Luna Park. And he tensed.

And she knew. The man must have run off in that direction, where the girls had surely gone. With the oxygen filling her lungs again, her mind cleared, and some of her strength returned. "We have to try to find them."

Before he did.

The bad man who'd been haunting the girls' nightmares for over a week now. The bad man who was intent on killing them because he knew that at least one of them had seen him kill Mrs. Miller.

How the hell had what was supposed to be such a simple job gotten so damn screwed up? Kill an old lady…

How hard could that be?

Actually that hadn't been that bad at all. He'd intended to make it look like a mugging. Kill her in an alley. Get her keys and search her damn apartment for anything incriminating.

Not to him but to his client.

Get rid of that just like he'd gotten rid of her.

But he hadn't easily gotten rid of her because there'd been damn witnesses. So he'd stolen that car and had tried running them down, but he'd missed them then. And in the parking garage, after watching the building for a week, he'd figured out the code residents had been punching into the gate. But even in the parking garage he'd missed them.

He chased them now, through the weeds and brush of an abandoned field, toward those lights. That must have been where the kids had headed.

He would have caught up with their little legs already if not for their mother. She had to be dead. He had to have choked the life out of her. But damn, she'd fought him hard.

He hurt all over, from the gunshot wound she'd reopened. And from that damn thing she'd hit him with.

His ears rang yet, but maybe that was because of firing his gun in that stairwell at the cop. Hell, that guy might have hit him, too.

He'd been so pumped, so impatient to catch those kids, that he might not have noticed the pain. Till now...

Now everything hurt. But he wasn't going to stop until he'd finished this. Until he'd gotten rid of those kids.

They'd seen his face. They were the only ones who had. He'd worn the mask after that, after his big mistake.

The closer he came to the park, the brighter the lights and the louder the music. It reverberated inside his head, making it ache even more than it had from her hitting him.

She damn well better be dead. But someone else had shown up, another guy with a gun. One that had had ammo in it. If only he'd had some in his...

Before getting any closer to the gates and risking anyone seeing him, he stopped, hiding in the relative shadows. He reached into his pocket and pulled out another clip and shoved it into his gun. This time he would be ready.

This time he would not miss.

He started forward, intent on finding his targets. And he nearly stumbled over a stuffed animal among the weeds. Maybe someone had won it in the park.

He stooped to pick it up, thinking of using it to lure the girls out.

But he didn't need to do that. All he had to do was get close enough to get a good shot. Two good shots. He wasn't going to rest until those little mini witnesses were dead.

Chapter 23

Cash hadn't wanted to bring Valentina with him, but he hadn't wanted to leave her alone and unprotected, either. In case the shooter hadn't left.

In case he hadn't gone after the girls.

But just like her, he was pretty damn sure that he had. As they neared the park, the darkness receded, illuminating the weeds and the stuffed bunny lying among them, blood staining its white fur.

Valentina grabbed it and gasped. "Oh, my God, he already found them…"

"We don't know that," Cash said, trying to give her hope even as his stomach lurched with dread. Those sweet little girls had to be all right. He couldn't have lost them just as he'd finally found them.

"Then why is there blood on Bunny?" she asked. "They weren't hurt."

Not like she was. Her neck was red, her voice raspy, and she limped beside him now that they weren't running like they had across the field.

She'd fought hard to protect them, to save them. She hadn't failed them, not like he had. He should have been there.

"The blood could be his," Cash pointed out. "He could be hurt."

She raised her hands, which had red smears on them. "He is…"

Damn. She was fierce. A fighter. And maybe their daughters were, too.

"They know he's a bad man," Cash reminded her. "They would run from him. And he won't just shoot them in the middle of a crowd. He's trying to kill them because he thinks they're witnesses…"

"To Mrs. Miller's murder," she finished when he trailed off. "They were. At least Ana was."

"As tragic as that is, it's good at the moment," Cash said. "They'll be so scared of him that they'll run. They'll hide from him." The question was where.

They walked up to the gates, and as they did, they could hear a commotion inside, voices raised, some screaming.

"He's here," Valentina breathed.

Cash flashed his shield at the gatekeeper. "Did you call the police?" he asked.

The young woman nodded. "When I saw the

man. He had a gun and is wearing a mask. And he's bleeding…"

Cash started inside, to track that blood like a hunter would track a wounded animal. But when Valentina followed him, he stopped. "You need to stay here, at the gate, wait for police."

She shook her head. "No. Those are my kids."

My.

Not *ours*. But then she had raised them alone until now. And even now…

She'd been the one with them tonight, the one getting them out of the burning building. The one fighting off a gunman to save them.

A professional killer…

Who didn't seem too damn professional right now, as if he'd lost his objectivity in his desperation. Or was he more afraid of whoever had hired him than he was of getting caught?

Either way, the guy had nothing left to lose at this point.

"Where would they go?" Cash asked her. Because she did know them best.

He barely knew them at all.

"They love the carousel."

"But they'd need tickets and they have no money."

"We come here so often, someone might let them on," she said, and she started limping toward that carousel.

Cash kept his gun steady in one hand while he slid his other arm around her, helping her, as they both hurried toward the ride with the music and lights. He didn't notice anyone standing around it but parents probably waiting for their kids. There was no bleeding man with a gun. Where the hell had he gone?

Had they gone?

"Where are they?" Valentina asked, her voice cracking with fear. "They would want to ride the horsey…"

"They would want to get away from the bad man," Cash said, hoping like hell that they had. "Where else? Where could they hide?"

"The bathrooms maybe…" Valentina murmured and she pulled away from him, heading toward the restrooms.

Maybe they would think they could hide from him in the woman's bathroom. Valentina pushed open the door and looked inside but shook her head. "They're not in there…"

They weren't the only ones who'd just disappeared. But then screams rang out again and people started running away from another attraction.

Valentina gasped. "The Fun House."

It made sense. Maybe they had been able to slip past the lines, to get inside, and hide. Hopefully Cash and Valentina would find them before the gunman did.

They ran toward the Fun House as other people ran from it, yelling, "Shooter! Shooter!"

He must have seen the kids go inside. He was already after them? Cash hadn't heard any gunshots yet.

People were still fleeing from the ride, running

out the back. Then gunshots reverberated from some-where inside it.

More people screamed and ran. Valentina was one of them, running toward the entrance instead of for the exit. Cash wanted to hold her back, but he knew that she would fight him as hard as she had the as-sassin if he tried. So he just stepped in front of her, entering first to the laughter of clowns and the flash of lights and the reflections of all the mirrors.

He moved ahead, keeping his body between her and the rest of the ride. "Ana! Luci!" he called out. "The bad man is in here so stay hidden!"

Gunfire rang out again, glass breaking around him. He ducked down and dragged Valentina down with him.

"Come out!" the guy yelled. "Come out or your mom and dad are dead, little girls!"

And in some of the unbroken mirrors, Cash caught the reflection of his daughters, their faces and bodies distorted and reflected back.

"No! Get down!" Valentina screamed. "Play dead!"

The man fired at those mirrors.

And Cash jumped up and fired back, striking him once. Twice. The guy dropped to the ground like Valentina had told their daughters to do. Had they done it in time?

Or had he hit them?

It was all over.

The bad man was dead. And the girls were not.

That should have been all that mattered to Valentina. They should have been all that mattered as they had been for the last three years.

But too much had happened.

She'd fallen in love with her ex-husband all over again. But no matter how many times he'd called her his wife over the past week, she was definitely his ex.

And after they'd taken the girls out of the Fun House and back to a safe place, a hotel suite close to the beach, she felt that it was over between her and Cash.

He'd helped her settle the girls down in the bedroom, but even as he'd read to them, he'd been distracted, as if his mind was elsewhere. As if they weren't the focus anymore...

Probably because they were no longer in danger, they were no longer a priority or a responsibility to him.

The girls were safe and sleeping in the bedroom of the hotel suite. And as Cash closed the door on that room, he turned toward her. "Are you sure you're all right?" he asked, his gaze focused on her neck.

It was sore, like her ankle, but nothing was broken. Nothing had been fractured beyond repair but maybe their relationship. And she didn't know why...

He'd been so concerned back at the building and the park. But maybe that was why he was shutting down now.

"I'm fine," she insisted. "You can leave."

He sucked in a breath and quietly asked, "You want me to go?"

"I can tell you have one foot out the door, just like you did for most of our marriage." And she'd fought too hard tonight to fight anymore. That was why she'd just signed those divorce papers three years ago. She didn't want to be with someone who wasn't going to make time for her in his life, and she certainly didn't want that for her daughters, either.

"Valentina…"

She waited for him to go on, but it was clear he didn't know what to say. And she was too tired.

"I do need to go back to the scene," he said. "I have to finish giving my statement to the investigating officers. Make sure that this is really over. I'll have an officer posted at the door of the hotel until we know for sure."

"How about Dave?" she asked with concern. She'd asked earlier, but they'd had no news of his condition at that time. The sergeant had still been in surgery.

He released a ragged sigh. "He's going to be okay," he said.

She emitted a shaky breath of her own. "That's good. He saved our lives." Cash had, too, after Dave got hit. "And you, you killed the guy. We're safe now." There was no reason for him to go back to the scene, to leave, except that he clearly didn't want to stay.

"He was a professional, Valentina. That means someone hired him."

She would have glared at him, if she'd had the energy. "I realize that. Someone hired him to kill Mrs. Miller. Not us. The only reason the assassin came after us was because he thought Ana and Luci could identify him. Maybe he even thought I'd seen him…" She might have glanced into that alley when she'd heard what had sounded like a car backfiring. But she'd been so distracted thinking of Cash's call that she hadn't realized it had even been a gunshot and she hadn't noticed anything. Not like Ana had.

"It's over," she said, and maybe she was trying to convince herself now. "Ana won't need to testify or give a statement."

He tensed. "She won't have to testify, but I'll have to see about the statement. That's why I should go back there."

"You should go back there," she agreed. "Because you don't want to stay. You don't want to be with us. You don't want that family any more now than you did three years ago."

He flinched, but he didn't argue with her, just as he hadn't when she'd moved out three years ago. "You're exhausted, and we shouldn't be having this conversation right now." He glanced toward the bedroom where the girls slept.

She didn't want their children to overhear them, either. But they were so exhausted that she doubted anything could wake them up, not even another fire alarm. "You don't want to have a conversation with me," she said. "Just as you didn't want to talk three years ago. You don't want to talk. You don't want to compromise. When are you going to realize that it doesn't have to be all or nothing? I'm not asking you to leave your job."

"It's more important than ever that I focus on the job now," he said. "With the Landmark Killer making a threat against Ashlynn."

She was dubious. "A real threat? Or did he just mention her?"

"He said that maybe she shouldn't be alive."

She gasped and pressed a hand to her mouth. Why was there so much evil, so much violence in the world? She respected and understood Cash's need to fight it, just as she'd fought for her girls tonight.

She was too tired to fight for her and Cash, though. And maybe so was Cash, especially since he already had another fight on his hands. "You need to go to Ashlynn. Protect her," she said, and she reached for the door to the hall, intending to show him out. Then she would crawl into the empty double bed next to the one the girls shared in the bedroom, and she would probably cry into her pillow until exhaustion claimed her. She was exhausted physically and emotionally right now.

"I…don't know where Ashlynn is," he said.

And her pulse quickened. "Oh, no! I'm sorry. You need to find her—"

"No, I need to find the Landmark Killer," he said. "Ashlynn went into hiding."

Valentina's pulse slowed a little then. "So she's safe…"

"Unless the Landmark Killer finds her before we find him," he said.

When a short time ago he'd seemed antsy and desperate to leave, now it was almost as if he was stalling. "You don't have to explain yourself to me," she said. "I understand why you need to leave. I know why your job is so important to you, especially now, with Ashlynn in danger."

"I want to make sure that you and the girls aren't in danger anymore either," he said. "I don't want anything to happen to you." Then finally he stepped through the door she'd opened for him and out into the hall.

She closed it behind him and leaned back against it. She should have told him that he was too late. That it had already happened; she was already hurt. And it wasn't her ankle or her throat.

It was her heart.

He'd broken it again.

Fury coursing through him, the Landmark Killer slammed his cell down onto the ground and barely resisted the urge to stomp on it, too. He'd been scrolling through the headlines, and all the local news, even some of the national news, was about the shooting at Coney Island's Luna Park but not *his* shooting.

Some nameless hired assassin was stealing all the news headlines from him. Just because he'd gone after some helpless little girls…

That made the man a coward who shouldn't get any mention at all in the news.

The Landmark Killer was the *hero*.

He was the brave one.

The smart one.

Just like Maeve O'Leary.

She knew what he was doing for her, that he was trying to free her. That he appreciated her. Did anyone appreciate him?

Did the FBI's special team respect him? How smart he was? While they were desperately trying to profile and figure out everything about him, he already knew everything about *them*.

About their murdered daddy...

About Cash's sad ex-wife. She was certainly sad now because after the Landmark Killer had sent Ashlynn that text, they were all going to focus on him again. Which they should have been doing...

Instead, first Brennan and then Cash had gotten distracted with their personal lives. Cash should have realized the first time his marriage failed that he couldn't make it work. He couldn't do anything but his job if he had any hope of catching someone as smart as the Landmark Killer. Cash hadn't even realized that the Landmark Killer had been in the parking garage with him at Cash's apartment that night.

Cash had turned with his gun, on edge because of his text. The texts he loved sending them. He was having so much fun messing with them, letting them know that he was smarter than they were. Even Ashlynn...

Chapter 24

Despite all his years in law enforcement, Cash had never been as scared as he'd been in that *Fun* House a week ago. He'd been so close to losing what mattered most to him. The gunman had been firing wildly, and Cash had had to take his shot, but in that moment, with all those mirrors reflecting back and contorting the killer's shadow and his daughters' images, he feared he might mistakenly shoot them instead of the bad man who'd been terrorizing them for more than a week.

And then he would be the bad man. Not just to them but to Valentina, too. But he'd wound up the bad man to her anyway because he hadn't known how to cope with the aftermath of that overwhelming fear he'd felt.

The fear that he would love and lose his family like he'd loved and lost his dad. To a serial killer...

And while the bad man hadn't been a serial killer, per se, he'd probably killed a lot of people. The FBI had already linked him to more murders than Maeve O'Leary and the Landmark Killer combined. But they hadn't yet linked him back to whoever had recently hired him to kill an old woman.

That made Cash uneasy. He wasn't entirely sure that his family was safe.

Not just Ashlynn, who'd gone so deeply underground that she couldn't be found, but his immediate family. The girls and Valentina.

She'd scared him nearly as much as that hired killer had. Because she'd just seemed so done with him, so tired. Of course, after what she'd been through, she'd had every reason to be. He was tired, too.

"Did you sleep here again?" Brennan asked as he walked into the conference room where Cash had been working. "You look like hell."

"I feel like hell," Cash admitted. He missed his girls. He missed his wife. He missed the family he'd vowed he'd never wanted. What a fool he'd been...

Not just three years ago but now as well. And he knew it; he just didn't know what to do about it.

"What are you doing?" Brennan asked.

"Working," he said. "We've got to find the Landmark Killer. He's threatened Ashlynn."

"And Ashlynn took measures to protect herself, which I suspect is what you're really doing."

"What do you mean?" Cash asked, his body tensing as his twin seemed to stare right inside him.

"Same thing I did for years, using you as my example, that there was no way to have a relationship while working this job, especially in this unit…" He gestured around the conference room where Cash had his laptop open and papers spread across the long table.

He glanced a little guiltily at those papers and the open files on his laptop. He was checking out Bradley Jones, one of the many aliases of the man he'd killed a week ago. The man who'd been trying to kill his family.

Cash was the one who'd done that himself when he'd walked away from them, leaving them alone at the hotel when all he'd really wanted to do was hold them close and never let them go. But the reality of how close he'd come to losing them had shaken him so badly…

"I was wrong," Brennan said. "And you are, too. Stella and I are happy, are making our relationship work for both of us. You could do that, not just for you and Valentina but for those little girls, too. You've already missed too much of their lives. What the hell are you doing here?"

"Trying to make sure they stay safe," Cash insisted. "You know someone hired that killer—"

"Not to kill them," Brennan said.

"That's what Valentina said," he admitted. "But I can't help feeling that it's not over. That's why when Ashlynn checked in the last time, I asked her to do a deep dive, see what she could dig up on the assassin, see if he had some way of keeping track of who had hired him. Like a safe-deposit box or a file on the cloud. Something."

"You sound pretty desperate to find something," Brennan said. "To prove your point?"

"To make sure my *family* is safe," Cash insisted.

"I don't think it's the killer that you're worried about," Brennan said. "I think you're scared of losing them, so instead you're pushing them away first so it's on your terms, something you can control."

Cash sucked in a breath as he felt his twin's words like a sharp jab. He hadn't realized just how well Brennan knew him, maybe better than Cash knew himself.

"Losing Dad was so hard on us," Brennan said. "Made us feel so helpless. That's why we do what we do. To take back some control."

"And to take it away from the killers, to bring them to justice," Cash insisted.

"Yes, true. We're saving people, but at what cost? Losing ourselves?" Brennan asked. He pointed to Cash, who could imagine how bad he looked.

He hadn't trimmed his hair or beard in…he didn't remember how long, and he hadn't slept more than an hour at a time for over a week. "How can you back away? How can you keep the job manageable?" Cash asked, and he really wanted to know.

"Remember that you're not doing it alone," Brennan said. "We're all in it together, in this unit—"

"Unless one of us is the Landmark Killer." And that was looking more and more likely.

"You know who you can trust," Brennan said. "Me, Patrick, Ashlynn. Valentina."

Could he, though? She'd kept his daughters from him, but he knew why, because she'd been afraid that he would do exactly what he'd done. That he would get close to them and then back away, breaking their hearts.

Like he'd broken hers?

His heart ached in his chest, feeling hollow and empty without them, without his family. He'd broken his own heart, too.

God, he missed them so damn much. He'd reached out every other day over the past week, texting Valentina to ask if the girls could FaceTime him. He'd missed seeing them, holding them, reading to them. Instead of answering his text, she'd just had the girls call him. He hadn't even seen her, just their sweet little faces.

They'd kept asking him when he was coming home. As if he lived with them. He had for a week, but he didn't think Valentina would have ever asked him to move in with them. Maybe it was because he'd told her three years ago that he couldn't live on Coney Island, that he had to stay close to the office because of cases like this when he'd worked around the clock.

But his twin was right. He needed to stop doing that. He needed to take control of his life and make sure that he had one. That he didn't burn himself out with work and lose what mattered most to him.

His family.

He could only hope that it wasn't too late…
That he hadn't already lost them.

Even a week after the threat against their lives was eliminated, Valentina was still exhausted. Since the fire had been confined to just that car in the parking garage, the smoke on the other levels of the high-rise had cleared and been cleaned up quickly. So she and the girls had been allowed to move back home a few days ago.

But it no longer felt like home to her or, she suspected, to the twins either, without their daddy there. They kept asking when he was coming home, and she didn't have the heart to tell them the truth.

Especially when she wasn't exactly sure what the truth was…

He'd been so strange after the shooting, so on edge, that she'd thought he couldn't wait to get away from them, to leave them again.

That the only reason he'd been with them had been to protect them from that threat, that assassin.

She shivered as she thought of him and glanced around the library. After closing, it was eerily quiet. She was the only one here, working late to make up for all the time she'd missed. The girls were with her parents, who'd checked them all into a hotel with a swimming pool. After learning how much danger they'd been in, Mom and Dad had paused their travels to come home to see them. While Valentina was happy her parents were in town, she wasn't happy about all the questions they kept asking her about Cash.

Because she couldn't answer those questions.

She'd thought he was going to let them go just as he'd let her go those three years, with not a word of contact until he'd called when he'd gotten that text from the Landmark Killer. The text about his sad ex-wife. But over the past week, he kept reaching out, talking to the girls. He'd even read them a story over the phone the other night.

A book he'd had delivered to the condo.

And the sound of his voice...

The gentle, loving way he spoke to their daughters had her falling for him all over again. No. She'd never fallen out of love with him, not three years ago and certainly not when he'd moved in to protect them. She'd just fallen deeper and deeper. Her heart ached for missing him.

She was certainly sad now.

But she was more than sad.

She was also mad.

At herself and at him.

They'd fought so hard to save their daughters from danger. Why hadn't they fought for each other like that?

Why hadn't she?

He was busy trying to stop a serial killer and track down who'd hired that terrible man to murder Mrs. Miller. What was she doing?

She'd put away the last of the books that had come in. So she turned her attention back to the one that had never gone out...

She'd found it sitting on her desk when she came

back, but she hadn't had the time or the wherewithal to look at it yet. It was the memoir she'd ordered for Mrs. Miller. Wanting a distraction from Cash, from the girls missing him, from her missing him, she picked up the book and began to read it.

The Broadway dancer hadn't just written about the famous people she'd met; she'd written about a powerful lover. A Mafia boss who'd treated her well while killing anyone else who'd crossed him. The memoir had been reprinted after the dancer's death and included a letter from the editor in the beginning that hinted at the dancer's death not being the mugging it had been made to look like but a cold-blooded murder. An act of revenge of that Mafia boss...

Valentina shivered at the similarity between that woman's death and the death of the woman who'd requested the copy of that memoir, who'd been writing her own. No. Mrs. Miller had been writing about people she'd known, more exciting and more famous people. She'd known the actress. Had she known her boyfriend, too? Suddenly Valentina knew who'd hired that assassin.

A very powerful man.

Of course she had no proof. Nobody had ever been able to get enough evidence or any willing witnesses to the man's crimes to put him in prison. He'd escaped justice for a long time, so long that he was an old man. He'd supposedly retired years ago, but the rumor around Brooklyn was that he was still in control behind the scenes.

She was suddenly very aware of how alone she

was in the library, which was dark but for the light in her office. Rattled, she closed the memoir and grabbed her purse. Usually she would have no issue walking home, even at this hour, but tonight she thought about calling an Uber.

Or Cash…

She had the perfect excuse to initiate contact, to tell him she'd solved his case for him. Of course she'd had to work overtime to do it, just as he so often worked overtime. No. He worked all the time.

Could she find a way to accept that? To take whatever time he had left?

Didn't she and the girls deserve more from him?

Frustrated, with herself and with him, she figured the walk home would be good to clear her head, so she could come up with a plan to fix her broken heart. And she doubted that man who'd hired the assassin knew anything about her or her girls. The killer had just been trying to eliminate the witnesses to his crime.

She locked the door behind her, and then she turned around on the sidewalk. And immediately she realized the mistake she'd made in not calling Cash.

A limo idled at the curb, a couple big men leaning against the side of it. And when they opened the back door, she knew who was waiting inside for her.

That very old, very powerful, very murderous old man…

Chapter 25

Cash wasn't sure if it was good luck or bad luck that he had a tendency to turn up just when Valentina needed him. Good luck on his part that he wasn't too late. Bad luck on hers that her life kept getting put in danger.

He knew he wasn't to blame this time, though. He knew who was; Ashlynn had found the evidence he was looking for. Then he'd tried to track down Valentina to tell her, and he found her just as she was coming out of the library to the men waiting for her.

As one of the big guys stepped forward to grab her, Valentina screamed and pulled a canister of pepper spray from her purse. While she raised that, Cash raised his gun.

"Stop!" he yelled, and he stepped out of the shadows into the light.

Valentina tensed as well as the men who reached beneath their jackets, as if they intended to pull their weapons and start firing at him.

"Special Agent Colton, FBI," he told them. "And I'm not alone. A warrant has been issued for your boss." Technically he wasn't alone since Valentina was there, armed with her pepper spray. But hopefully they would think that he wouldn't come by himself to serve a warrant to a Mafia boss. "We already have proof of one murder. I don't think he wants to add any more charges against him, especially of a federal agent."

The guys glanced from him through that open door to the man who sat in the back seat. Cash held his breath, hoping that he wouldn't be forced into another shoot-out. While he waited, he edged between that car and Valentina, using his body to protect her.

The guys took their hands from beneath their jackets and turned back around to face Cash. "We will be waiting for you at FBI headquarters with legal representation."

The old man said something, and one of the guys chuckled. "Unless you'd like a ride, Special Agent Colton."

God, he was brazen, but then he'd gotten away with his crimes for so many years that he probably didn't believe he would ever be prosecuted. And he probably wouldn't have been caught this time if he hadn't had to go after one little old lady. The assassin he'd hired to kill her had been confused about the old man's motive, too, confused enough that he'd gotten some more details out of him, details that Bradley Jones or whoever he really was had recorded and uploaded to the cloud.

He was actually going to go down for more than one murder.

But at least one of those would not be Valentina's. When the men got into the limo and it pulled away from the curb, Cash finally released that breath he'd been holding.

"Are you just going to let him drive off?" Valentina asked him as she gripped his arm, turning him around to face her. "He's probably heading straight to the airport to leave the country, to someplace with no extradition."

"Probably," he agreed. "But there will be agents at the airport to stop him. There really is a warrant for his arrest."

"You know?" she asked, her dark eyes wide with surprise.

"Obviously you do," he said.

She nodded. "I finally read the book Mrs. Miller had asked me to track down for her. She'd said it was about a friend of hers, and that she wanted to write about these friends. I think she intended to expose him in her own memoir for the murder of an actress she knew and that he had dated."

"Yes, that's exactly what she intended to do. Unfortunately she let that slip when she was talking to people about her memoir."

"The wrong people," Valentina said.

"But you didn't know before, did you?"

She shook her head now. "No. I would have told you." But her face flushed slightly.

And he pointed out, "You didn't call me when you found out."

She released a shaky sigh. "I thought about it. But lucky for me you have a habit of turning up when I'm in danger."

"That's not the only time I want to turn up, Valentina," he said, his heart overflowing with love for her. "I want to do more than protect you and the girls. I don't want to be with you just when you're in danger. I want to be with you always."

And now he held his breath again, waiting for *her* reply this time.

Valentina hadn't intended to keep Cash waiting for her answer, but his cell had started ringing. And then police and other FBI agents had shown up on the sidewalk as suddenly and unexpectedly as the limo and Cash had appeared. Apparently some agency or another had had the Mafia boss under surveillance and had reported what had happened.

And then she and Cash had had to give reports to those officers and agents. Sometime, during the course of those interviews, she'd lost track of him, and an officer had driven her back to the condo.

She hadn't had the chance to talk to him again, to answer that question, although it had actually been more of a statement than a question. *I want to be with you always.*

Instead of making her happy, the words filled with her sadness. It felt like another promise he couldn't keep, like the ones he'd made her when they got married.

He'd made promises to the girls, too, though, about keeping them safe, about protecting them from the bad man. And that promise he had kept.

He'd protected and saved them.

Could he keep this promise, too, if she gave him the chance?

Dare she give him a chance?

If she had the chance for that family she'd always wanted, the one she'd had that week that Cash had lived with them, was she selfish and cowardly not to take it just because she was afraid of getting hurt?

Pain and disappointment were parts of life, but so were joy and contentment. Without risking one, was the other possible? Probably not for her...

Not when love led her back to the man who'd hurt her before. But she would rather risk him hurting her again than live without him the way she had the past three years.

She would rather take whatever time he could give her and the girls around his work than never see him at all. Realizing that led her to another realization, that she had been as unwilling as he'd been to compromise before.

She'd wanted more instead of appreciating what she'd had, what he'd given her. The love. Their babies...

Tears rushed to fill her eyes, and she closed them. When she opened them, the elevator doors were opening to her floor. She was home, but it didn't feel like home right now, and that wasn't just because her girls were with her parents.

It was because Cash wasn't here.

She shouldn't have left with the officer. She should have waited for him. But she hadn't even known if he was still at the local police precinct or if he'd left without her.

Maybe he'd had to go back to the FBI office. Or maybe...

Maybe she hadn't answered him fast enough, and he'd thought she wasn't interested in a future with him.

She could call him once she got into her condo. She quickly unlocked her door to step inside, but once the door creaked open, she had a strange sensation that the place wasn't as empty as it was supposed to be.

That someone was here, waiting for her.

She reached into her bag again for that canister of pepper spray she was so glad she carried. But before she could pull it out, she heard a little giggle. Another one echoed it, and she smiled.

"Do I hear some mice?" she wondered aloud. "Or is that a robber?"

A light flickered on: a candle. Then another and another...

"We're not robbers, Mommy," Ana solemnly told her.

"We 'prising you," Luci said with a smile.

"You certainly are," Valentina assured them. But the biggest surprise of all wasn't their being here. She'd thought they might not want to spend the entire night away from home after just being able to come back a few days ago.

The biggest surprise was that it wasn't her mom and dad with them but Cash. He'd lit the candles on the dining room table and some on the kitchen counter and another on an end table.

Along with the candles were flowers and a couple of balloons that she suspected the girls had chosen since one said Happy Birthday and another Get Well Soon.

They really loved balloons.

"Wow," she said. "I definitely wasn't expecting this."

"Daddy planned it."

"That was quick," Valentina said.

"I was surprised earlier at the library," Cash said. "I wasn't expecting that. I thought I would be walking with you back here, once your mom and dad told me you were working late."

"You already had this planned?" she asked. "Before that…?" So his showing up when he had hadn't been just another coincidence. Maybe divine intervention. She shuddered thinking what might have happened.

"Definitely someone looking out for us," Cash said as if he'd read her mind. "Maybe your grandparents."

She smiled, thinking of how happy they'd been,

how in love. She could see that. "But since you have a habit of turning up right when I need you, I think it could be your dad…"

He tensed for a moment, as he usually did when someone brought up his dad. But then he grinned and nodded. "Maybe it is. Then hopefully he's looking out for all of us, not just me."

Ashlynn was still in danger. Because the Landmark Killer hadn't been caught, a lot of people were still in danger. But yet Cash was here instead of at work, and apparently he'd been here before going to the library to see her.

"This is quite a surprise," she said, gazing around at the candles and flowers. There was even a pizza box sitting on the counter, from their favorite place. It wasn't even in Coney Island, so he must have picked it up earlier or paid extra to have it delivered here.

"A pleasant one?" Cash asked. "Could you get used to coming home to me every night?"

Her pulse quickened. "Is that what you meant when you said earlier that you want to be here always?"

He nodded. "I'm not quitting my job or anything—"

"I don't want you to," she assured him. "I know how important it is…"

"Catching bad guys," Ana finished for her when she trailed off.

She nodded. "Yes." He'd saved more lives than just hers and the girls with the bad people he and his unit had brought to justice. "I never wanted you to give it up," she told him. And maybe she hadn't made that clear enough; maybe she hadn't been understanding enough.

He stepped closer to her. "I know. You just wanted me to get my priorities straight. And they are now. You and our family, you're all my number one priority. And I'm just sorry I didn't realize that three years ago."

The tears rushed up on her again, making her nose wrinkle as she tried to hold them back. "I should have tried harder. Fought like I did for the girls and me that night…"

"Tonight, too," he said. "You're fierce and fearless."

"Not fearless enough to fight for what I want."

"What do you want, Valentina?"

"You. Our family."

He dropped to his knees then. And the little girls giggled and started climbing on him. He grinned. "Maybe I should have tackled this part alone…"

She shook her head. "No, this is perfect." And it was, even with the Happy Birthday and Get Well Soon balloons and all those flickering candles making her worry that the smoke alarm might go off again.

"Valentina Acosta Colton, I love you. I have always loved you and I always will. So will you have mercy on me and forgive me for not fighting for us three years ago? And will you give me a chance to spend the rest of our lives making that up to you? Will you marry me all over again?"

Her heart was beating so fast with excitement and love. "You have nothing to make up to me. I kept expecting you to compromise, and I wasn't willing to do that myself. I promise you now that I will always meet you at least halfway. That I will be the partner I promised to be six years ago, when we got married the first time."

"So is that a yes?" he asked, his green eyes shining with love and happiness.

"Yes, I love you!" She leaned down and pressed her lips to his.

And the girls danced around them both.

"She said yes!" Luci announced.

"She said yes!" Ana echoed.

And then Valentina's parents were there, too, and someone had a cell with Cash's mom FaceTiming on it, offering her congratulations as well.

But as quickly as they'd all shown up, they were gone again. His mom and her parents and the girls whom they'd whisked back to the hotel, leaving Valentina and Cash alone together again.

"I'm sorry," he said, his voice gruff with emotion.

"I am, too," she said. "I am as responsible as you are for what happened three years ago. More, maybe, because I didn't tell you when I found out I was pregnant. I'm surprised you've been able to forgive me for that." Surprised and blessed.

"I love you so much that I could forgive you anything," he said. "But I also understand why you did that. All those times I told you that I didn't want to be a father..." His voice cracked. "I can't believe what a fool I was. I can't imagine a world without them in it. That was what hit me so hard the night that hit man came after them in the Fun House, after nearly choking you to death." He shuddered. "I was so scared that I was going to lose the people I love the most."

"But you withdrew…"

"To protect myself," he said. "To try to deny that feeling of helplessness and fear…"

And suddenly she understood him so well. He must have felt so helpless when his dad died and then that horrible night in the Fun House…

She wrapped her arms around him, holding him close. "I'm sorry."

"Let's put that all behind us from here on," he proposed. "We can't undo what we did or didn't do. Let's move forward, if that's what you really want." He studied her face now, his green eyes so intense. "That was what I was just apologizing for, putting you on the spot, proposing to you in front of them. I didn't give you a chance to tell me, privately, how you really feel. I was fighting for us, and that was fighting dirty."

"It was," she agreed.

And he flinched.

"But I'm happy that you care enough to fight right now," she said.

"I love you so much," he said. "I always have, but how do you really feel?"

"Like fighting," she said.

And he drew back as if he was expecting a blow.

"For us, too," she said. "I love you so much, Cash.

I've missed you so much. I can't imagine my life without you in it. And because of that I will keep fighting. For us. For our family. For our love."

He lifted her up and spun around with her clasped tightly in his arms. "With as fierce as you are, I have no worries that we'll be together forever."

She wrapped her arms around his neck and pulled his head down for her kiss. "Forever," she promised him. And that was a promise she had every intention of keeping.

It felt like forever. Since Ashlynn had gone into hiding. Since he'd killed…

It had only been a little over a week. But it felt longer.

And he felt weaker, like his plan was beginning to fall apart. He had to claim the next life. An O to begin spelling out O'Leary. He couldn't wait much longer to take another life. Or to find her.

Ashlynn Colton was not smarter than him. She was not going to escape him…without one hell of a fight.

* * * * *

#2251 COLTON'S MONTANA HIDEAWAY
The Coltons of New York • by Justine Davis

FBI tech expert Ashlynn Colton's investigation into one serial killer has made her the target of another one. Only the suspect's brother—handsome Montana cowboy Kyle Slater—will help. But as the duo grows closer, their deadly investigation isn't the only thing heating up...

#2252 LAST CHANCE INVESTIGATION
Sierra's Web • by Tara Taylor Quinn

Decorated detective Levi Greggs just closed a high-profile murder case and took a bullet in the process. But when his ex-fiancée, psychiatrist Kelly Chase, returns to town with another mystery, saying no isn't an option. Searching the wilderness for a missing child reignites long-buried desire...and more danger than they bargained for.

#2253 HER SECRET PROTECTOR
SOS Agency • by Bonnie Vanak

Marine biologist Peyton Bradley will do anything to regain her memory and finish her important work. Even trust former navy SEAL Gray Wallace, her ex-bodyguard. Gray vows to protect Peyton, even as he falls for the vulnerable beauty. But will the final showdown be with Peyton's stalker, her family, her missing memory or Gray's shadowy past?

#2254 BODYGUARD MOST WANTED
Price Security • by Katherine Garbera

When his look-alike bodyguard is murdered, CEO Nicholas DeVere knows he'll be next. Enter security expert Luna Urban. She's not Nick's doppelgänger, but she's determined to solve the crime and keep the sexy billionaire safe. If only they can keep their arrangement all business...

Get 3 FREE REWARDS!

We'll send you 2 FREE Books plus a FREE Mystery Gift.

FREE Value Over **$20**

Both the **Harlequin Intrigue®** and **Harlequin® Romantic Suspense** series feature compelling novels filled with heart-racing action-packed romance that will keep you on the edge of your seat.

HARLEQUIN
PLUS

Try the best multimedia
subscription service for romance
readers like you!

Read, Watch and Play.

Experience the easiest way to get
the romance content you crave.

Start your **FREE TRIAL** at
<u>www.harlequinplus.com/freetrial</u>.